BANNED

FROM

TINDER

BANNED FROM FROM TINDER:

A Memoire

Hannah Evanstead

Hannah Evanstead
Honolulu, HI
www.bannedfromtinder.com
hannah@bannedfromtinder.com

ISBN
979-8-9887348-2-6 (Hard Cover)
979-8-9887348-1-9 (Paperback)
979-8-9887348-0-2 (eBook)

To Kyle.

I don't want to work another 10 minutes, either bro.

Table of Contents

PROLOGUE

A note on the contents of this novel:

If you know me, or think you know me...

No, you don't.

If you think one of these stories is about you, or someone you know...

No, it's not.

Similarities are purely coincidental.

In a world where life imitates art, and the truth is stranger than fiction, this is a memoire based loosely on real life events that happened to a real person–the author–names and places have been changed to preserve anonymity.

CHAPTER 1

INVISIBILITY

It is May when I finally find the courage to say the words. They tumble from my mouth and splash into our bedroom like icebergs calving from glaciers in the arctic. "I'm done! We are getting divorced." My heart is racing, and I feel it beating in my throat. I am beyond angry but the words, for as violent as they are, come quickly to rest in icy stillness. I have rehearsed them a million times in my head over the years, sometimes fantasizing, or perhaps strategizing, to tell him on a quiet night lying in bed when we aren't fighting, and things feel good. I can casually tell him then, rather than risk telling him during an argument, but this argument is different.

No one is yelling, it is just me stating facts, and his agreement. He is knowingly and intentionally being cruel to me, yet again, on Mother's Day no less, because he enjoys it, immensely. It is such pleasure for him to make me invisible, miserable, repeatedly, every day, but especially on Mother's Day. He offers no explanation other than his own enjoyment, and suggests he never means for me to take it personally, but he really doesn't like me and never has. For 15 years, ten of them as the mother to his children, we live like this. The invisibility is the worst part.

It takes a few months to pull the paperwork together after a brief attempt at therapy and a few weeks of consideration. In early July after a difficult Fourth of July camping trip with the kids, the paperwork is complete and ready to file. The ongoing response to the COVID pandemic prevents me from entering the building where he works, so I call him to come downstairs to the back entrance of the historic building when I arrive. I ask him to bring a notary from his office along to witness the signatures. We both know her as a spin instructor at our gym; it's unnecessarily awkward as we sign, and she notarizes the documents. I drive to the courthouse with the notarized petition for divorce and slide the documents through a makeshift delivery slot in the door. COVID has closed the courthouse, too.

We are officially done. I am exhilarated and terrified in equal measure. I am free to pursue happiness and a life worth living, which includes navigating the dating scene in 2020 during the peak of a global pandemic, at a time when isolation is recommended. The trouble is, I am already post-menopausal and suffer with the uniquely troublesome issues of an aging woman's body. Despite being a young, and otherwise healthy 43-year-old, sex is a "use it or lose it" activity and I have no intention of losing it, so in mid-July, a few days after filing the divorce petition, I log on to Tinder and set up my first profile. I use my laptop, so the app won't be on my work phone, which, at the time, is my only phone line.

CHAPTER 2

VISIBILITY

It is instant, like the moment lava flows into the ocean and turns to shiny black glass, a steady constant stream of hot, young bodies appear for my approval. They commingle within a sea of men my own age, most of whom have not cared well for themselves. The latter appear slovenly, overweight, unshaven, ungroomed, with unreasonable demands for women who, if exist are far out of their league – I swipe left. The former are breathtakingly stunning, mostly in their mid-twenties – I swipe right and they are all instant matches. I don't understand what they see in me, but they're eager.

The very first profile card though is my husband, grinning into the camera from his work desk. He is wearing the heavy winter gear of deep February in the Midwest, as if his profile is far older than the few hot July days since the divorce petition was filed with the court. He appears again occasionally over the next 18 months as I swipe for visibility – matching and linking, random at first and then with laser focus when I find the sweet spot. I burn through hot, young bodies for sport. Surprising them, when they think I am their fetish, only to find out they are mine. Sometimes my soon-to-be ex-husband's profile features updated photos showing him in the new condo I help him buy during the divorce, sometimes he poses with our kids. Often, he suggests he is traveling to his hometown when he doesn't have the kids and wants to share his weekend and his hotel room with anyone willing.

I know from the first time I see his card – if I can see his, he can see mine. And I look good. Confident, fit, sexy. Radiantly visible, with an ice-cold bio: *feelings are gross, don't catch them with me*. Eventually, my bio evolves to include more details, informed by the experiences of matching, usually – but not always – linking, and the delicate aftermath where men discover my tag line is no joke. No one spends the night. And the privilege to see me again is reserved for only the very best lovers. I swipe almost compulsively, usually left, but sometimes right when the aesthetics are appealing – and almost every time, it is an instant match. In the beginning, I don't know rejection.

By September the following year my bio evolves to include a list of disclaimers:

> *I want your hoodie.*
> *Feelings are gross; don't catch them with me.*
> *Professional left-swiper.*
> *I'm dating myself so you losers don't have to.*

#RageSober

I don't have WhatsApp and no, you can't have my phone number.

Snapchat is where my matches go to die.

Side note: why do men my own age have to be so old?

Ladies, I'm mostly looking for a threesome partner.

When I hit 700 matches, I delete this app and start over.

It's close #SorryNotSorry

Tinder, and the other dating apps that follow when I am banned from the platform in January 2022, are affectionately dubbed the "dick faucet" by a jilted lover. Because not only am I visible to my soon-to-be ex-husband, but I am visible, seen, and desired by all sorts of men, on all sorts of dating platforms. All of them intrigued and eager to meet me in real life. They track down my social media profiles, sometimes with alarming ease.

My inbox explodes with countless versions of "hey" or "gm beautiful" with only a very few creative pickup lines. I respond to nearly all of them anyway, almost as compulsively as I swipe, even when I am unsure. Once in the Fall of 2020, an uncertain swipe results in a flyover of a disc golf course on a hemp farm. I helped plant the crop earlier in the spring while I was cultivating a life for myself outside of my marriage – a demand of the soon-to-be ex-husband who wanted us to find our own friends and activities. We played disc golf as a family at the farm before the divorce and when the owner posts on social media for volunteers to help plant the crop in May of 2020, the timing is impeccable. I jump at the opportunity to get involved with the operation and spend the early spring quietly cultivating my feelings in the warm soil. We plant 7,000 CBD plants over five acres and spend the spring and summer maintaining the crop, so my friends are in the field when we fly over.

When the pilot offers me a flight as a first date in September of the same year, I can't say no and he is happy to have a nearby flyover target. Despite the circumstances, I don't join the mile high club, foolishly thinking this man might call me back for another adventure. He may be wealthy enough to own a plane and fly around the U.S. visiting relatives, but he isn't particularly handsome, and the date is a hard sell. I would have said no, if not for the flight, and he probably knows it. I never see him again. There are certainly more matches, and links, awaiting reply, many with far more sex appeal, and often far less of everything else – intelligence, careers, and conversation skills are among things I learn most young men lack, especially the ones I meet on Tinder.

❖❖❖❖❖❖

I create Tinder profiles and accumulate hundreds of matches, repeatedly deleting it and starting over when it becomes unmanageable. The first time, in July 2020, my aim is to *cultivate a few solid matches I can see on a regular basis*, as my earliest bio states after the *feelings are gross; don't catch them with me* tagline that remains my constant intro. When I have a good rotation going in the winter of 2020, I delete my Tinder profile for the first of many times. But from July to December 2020, there is the clumsy process of choosing which matches to chat with, which ones to share my socials or phone number with, and who to actually meet in real life. Then there is the chaotic bid to find times and places to link up that work around my odd family dynamic of cohabitating while the divorce works its way through the court system.

We take turns traveling with our kids on the weekends to give each other space. I know he has seen my profile when he demands that I not ever link with anyone in our family home. As part of the divorce settlement, he is expecting me to live in our family home with our kids to give them the stability of staying in their own home, while he rents a studio nearby and offers to spend his weeks with the kids in our home while I "make myself scarce." In August, I ask a realtor to put a For Sale sign in the front yard.

The first match I meet is a cute young fella with stunning blue eyes and blonde hair; he has no name, none of them do at first. He is overeager–a red flag I quickly learn to avoid. He comes to our home, with the For Sale sign out front, while the soon-to-be ex-husband is out of town for the weekend with our kids. The link is fast, he only lasts about 90 seconds after spending way too long finding his erection, and he smells like a musty combination of sweat and bologna. Hardly worth the effort, or argument that follows with my soon-to-be ex-husband. He explodes with anger because I take down the security cameras while he's gone and make up an excuse for their temporary disconnection. I can do better.

After that first link, I take the cameras down and disconnect them permanently, which opens the opportunity to meet at the house. As he comes to terms with the idea of buying a condo, he starts to lay claim on various furniture items, particularly our king size bed. Once again, he demands I keep my hookups out of the house, and out of his bed. He packs up the kids on his weekends and travels with them to see his relatives leaving the house empty and lonely.

These early matches are an odd mix of meeting in hotels, going to random homes and apartments, and the occasional link in our house with the For Sale sign out front. Aside from the challenges with the divorce, co-parenting while cohabitating, and work associate with the sale of the house, I am drowning in responsibilities at my actual job. There is very little time available for these encounters, so they are carefully nestled into my schedule between meetings and obligations to the kids. Timeliness is essential and I offer each one just a brief window, usually 30 to 60 minutes, to have their way with me.

They are all bad in the beginning. I meet a man at a hotel downtown when he is in town for a sports related conference. I park on the street, where my spouse will surely see my car if he walks between the two nearby buildings where he works. I meet this match in the hotel lobby. Covid conditions require masks in the lobby and elevator. He awkwardly kisses me through the mask on the way up to his room and we giggle about how silly it is but when we get into the room and take our clothes off, he keeps his mask on. He lasts more than two minutes, only barely, which turns out to be an all-too-common theme that ties many of these stories together. More often than not, they finish before I even get started. At least he has recently showered and smells faintly of soap instead of sweat.

On another occasion, with high expectations, I meet a doctor in his downtown hotel room. A giant dog greets me when I arrive and awkwardly watches as we link. It's cold and impersonal, and while he manages to last a while, it isn't particularly enjoyable or skillful. The dog jumps on the bed to snuggle with us afterwards. When I leave to return to my desk he starts messaging and calling me incessantly via Snapchat. He wants me to come back to do ketamine and coke with hookers he apparently also met on Tinder. I decline and eventually block him when he won't stop calling.

Then there is a businessman who is obsessed with feet and shoes, particularly a woman's business flats. He is desperate to play out his fantasy of smelling feet, especially in stockings, and shoes in a sexual situation without shame – weird, but I actually appreciate his candor and honesty about what he likes. I come to learn that we all like what we like, and among consenting adults, there is no shame in having preferences and desires outside of the norm. I love when people feel free enough to be pure and authentic in themselves.

After a few tries matching and some hot chatter about his fantasies, we finally connect. He comes to the house with the For Sale sign out front. He can't find his erection anywhere, despite smelling the shoes and my stocking feet and the requested foot job. After 15 miserable, distressing minutes of failure, he dresses and sheepishly shows himself out without a word. He isn't the last person to suffer with performance anxiety, but he is the saddest, and the air is thick with shame as he navigates his way from our master suite on the second floor to the front door where he slips his shoes on and disappears in a black luxury sedan.

I always try to be kind and gentle when this happens, which often (but not always) leads to eventual success, but he isn't receptive and leaves abruptly. It is alarmingly common for links to be unable to perform, or to finish so quickly it hardly counts, but when they are good, they are amazing, and it's divine.

❖❖❖❖❖

There is a subjective and somewhat arbitrary factor that fuels swiping right or left when something stands out in a profile. This is how I encounter some of these more unusual links. For a while, I swipe right on all the disc golfers since I am an avid player. This eventually leads to hilarity. However, early on, the swiping is random, and often purely aesthetic. I swipe right on one Young Man, only 24 years old, because his profile specifies that he believes strongly in the oxford comma and wants to discuss that specific piece of punctuation. I love the oxford comma and the funny situations that have unfolded over the years when its omission has had legal or social consequences. I spend entirely too much time at work adding them into colleagues' client- or public-facing documents. I have to connect with him.

We meet at his apartment on the west side of town, opposite where I live in the house with the For Sale sign. We take bong rips and exchange Tinder stories beforehand, which I promise we will do early in our chats. He lasts no more than 30 seconds. We spend more time afterwards doing the same thing in comfortable repose on his couch. He is the blondest boy with the bluest eyes and longest white lashes I have ever seen, with a trim, muscular frame. He is an unusually pleasant match given the poor performance. He gives me a hoodie as a consolation prize, which I proceed to hang on my office chair in the house with the For Sale sign. A subtle jab at my soon-to-be ex-husband. Oxford and I still exchange messages and laugh about our awkward encounter. We keep each other updated on our professional trajectories and love lives. Eventually, he agrees to edit this manuscript to ensure proper punctuation throughout. I think he is just anxious to know what I've written about him.

Eventually, and finally, I match someone with whom the casual chitchat and banter on Tinder becomes a lifeline. Quickly moving to text, the mysterious Sir V captivates my imagination with smooth talk of sexual domination. He isn't a "Dom" or an "alpha" and doesn't come bearing a label or title. He is simply dominant by nature. It is impossible to do anything but submit.

We exchange messages constantly for days and finally agree he will come to the house with the For Sale sign during a planned open house to feign interest as a buyer. He wants to peer into my life, run his hand along the bed where I sleep, view my wardrobe in the closet. It is incredibly intimate and exciting. He comes back later that evening when I am home alone.

Our connection is explosive, the first time is a bit of a letdown after the heat of our text exchanges. As we lay in bed afterwards and he admits to being nervous. For hours he strokes my hair and rubs my back and legs, a warm haptic extension of our ongoing text conversation (which continue to this day). A second mind-blowing link follows. It leaves us both breathless and begging for more.

We agree, no matter what happens between us, we'll preserve a positive framework, and if ever we part ways, we do so as friends and lovers. Never as enemies and with no animosity. We meet several more times over the fall of 2020, at his place though, exploring the limits of our natural dom/sub connection. Always under the pretext where I do not know his name, but he knows mine.

Each time indulging in each other for hours on-end afterwards. We unpack our lives a little at a time with the knowledge that we can't and shouldn't be in a relationship when we are both so tender and raw from our prior partners. We are also somehow certain we are meant for each other. We re-match on Tinder with each new profile, even after we shift away from sexual encounters. It's a smooth transition to a strictly friendship-oriented connection where we offer support and camaraderie as fellow online dating warriors with unusual proclivities.

Our authenticity sets us free to accept ourselves as we are, and to honor our truth in every encounter. Especially the unusual ones. He changes his Facebook name to a fake name so we can be friends online while maintaining that novel little element of anonymity where I do not know his name. In the winter of 2021, we get matching tattoos on our wrists, and in September of 2022, to celebrate our two-year anniversary, he tells me his real name. It is, however, around the time we first meet–September 2020–when I gain traction.

CHAPTER 3

TRACTION

It starts with Sir V, and then there are more: The First, The Best, The Honest, Mr. NFL, Mr. Sunday, Mr. Massage, the Short Guy, The Gold Standard, and a variety of others. Many of them evolve to be my regulars in the fall of 2020. Some persist to this day, while others are just single encounters that redefine everything.

These matches have names. They have times (or at least one time) that work well for both of us. They have patterns of showing up. And they devour me in ways that no one else ever has. They are all young Black men, 26 to 28 years old, many of them fitness models and professional or semi-professional athletes, glossy in their appearance–with designer clothes, diamonds, lined up fades, nice cars. This is the sweet spot. I am shocked that they even notice me. What do they see in a 43-year-old divorcee with kids? It doesn't matter, I am visible–edible–and I like it. I love it. I can't get enough, and neither can they.

The first Black man I ever link with drives a big panel truck. He parks on a nearby street, and I pick him up in my car. We go to the house with the For Sale sign out front. He is clean, casually well-dressed, tall, and extremely fit. With long legs and arms, virtually no body fat, and eyes that are slightly too big for his sockets. He is unconventionally handsome, a fitness model and personal trainer, alongside numerous other business ventures. His skin is smooth and dark, and he smells faintly of the coconut oil he uses to moisturize his skin and hair. The sex is amazing. We continue to link frequently into the new year. Moving our links from the house with the For Sale sign to the new house I purchase as the court date to finalize the divorce nears.

He is plagued by insecurity though. Always asking if he looks good (he does), if he is good at it (he is), if others are better (some of them are), if his dick is big enough (it is on the larger side). All the while he also talks about wanting a dick-enlargement procedure (ok, weird, which I typically appreciate, and certainly won't judge). He obsesses over whether anyone else I link with is bigger than his rather impressive 9-inches (of course, some are). His need for validation becomes exhausting, an indication that our connection has run its course.

Holding no ill-will towards him, I still invite him to join the swinger's group to which I belong so he can attend a party. I let him know I will be there with the

Gold Standard (more on him later). It's not clear why he has a problem with the event but for some reason, he thinks it is some sort of dick contest. Apparently, he feels insecure that the Gold Standard is also a young Black man with a big dick. Never mind the dozens of other entirely average men in attendance.

The Gold Standard regularly accompanies me to events so most of the people already know him, and treat him like a friend, with one of my girlfriends coaxing him into briefly flashing himself. The First One is new to the group and struggles to interact with the crowd while resisting my attempts to mingle. When he sees the Gold Standard show himself, it initiates his dramatic exit. He leaves early after pulling me aside and throwing a fit I never quite understand. We never speak again, and after a few awkward online encounters, I block him on all platforms.

The Best link in this whole story is a one-time encounter that takes place in a lake-side condominium. The apartment is immaculate, with a perfectly appointed grey interior. He is stunning beyond compare. Well over six feet tall, a fitness model, personal trainer, and personal finance expert with huge muscles rippling through his warm, dark skin. He has a slight gap between his front teeth when he smiles. We exchange hot messages for a few days to establish a rapport where he understands I want to be put on a pedestal, worshiped, and devoured. No strings attached.

When I arrive at his condo, I tell him he has 75 minutes before I have to return to work. He uses every one of the minutes to pleasure me beyond any comparison. He takes a momentary break to carry me into his bedroom for a second, eruptive session of pure ecstasy, after first evoking a peak of euphoria on his living room's grey ottoman.

He lays me in his bed, and I ask if we are cuddling. He whispers into my ear a reminder that I asked him not to waste my time and the 75 minutes have not yet elapsed. He kisses his way from my ear to my pleasure center. He holds my hips firmly in place to persist while I writhe in response, waiting for him to take me one more time. Eventually, I beg for him to rise up and finish. He responds with one hand gently and expertly around my throat. The other pins my arms over my head. My body pitches underneath him as I try to consume his essence. His whole body thrusts into contractions as he finishes. We fall apart exhausted and happy. To this day, it remains the best sexual experience I've ever had.

We exchange a few messages afterward but never reconnect. I even message him when I move out of town two years later to no avail. I would have seen him every day for the rest of my life to be put on that pedestal again, but he has other plans. The encounter is seared into my memory like he touched my soul with a red-hot branding iron. It set a high bar for quality encounters that has not yet been matched, even though there have been some admirable contenders.

Like a drug, I chase that high, and like a drug, it's elusive to find a comparable experience and it's a dangerous pursuit. I am left feeling convinced now I can never settle for less from a partner. If I should ever recover enough to be in a relationship again, I need to find a man like him. But one who is available and for whom the interest is mutual, which turns out to be difficult to find.

The Honest connection is from Sierra Leone. He is one of many international lovers I take over the course of my life reclamation, or whatever it is that is happening. Despite his heritage, he is only average in size. A lesson in stereotypes, so to speak, but dark, strong, and unbearably handsome. His accent is barely discernible but characteristic of the British colonized countries of Africa. It lilts in my memories of him. He is studying sex positive books like the "The Ethical Slut" in an attempt to find an open relationship where he can be loved, in love, and a lover to many women.

We discuss the merits of being solopoly, a term for the relationship model where you are your own partner and your lovers, whether one or many, are secondary to the relationship with oneself. It's the modality I believe I'm following with myself in the center of a universe of men who fall to my feet for an opportunity to be in my bed. Even when that's all they really want.

The Honest one is admirable in skill, and the sex is worthy of many repeat visits, ebbing off only after he finds a girlfriend the following year. We meet for breakfast one last time after that and discuss his sex-positive future. He tells me he aspires to be like me, as free as I am, with many partners from which to choose on any given day. He also wants to remain in a relationship with his current girlfriend who is respectively vanilla – without a similar interest in alternative relationship models. Despite his admiration of my circumstances, the confidence with which I seek pleasure masks a deep-seated desire for true love and affection that remain elusive – a detail I only see in retrospect.

Mr. NFL is a gift. We match, even though he is in another state, and chat a little before landing on a date where I know I will be traveling close enough for us to meet. It is almost a month away though, so my expectations are not high. Normally, I would never travel for a first meeting, but I'll be playing a disc golf tournament in a nearby city and decide to make a weekend of it with a hotel the night before the event. We seize the opportunity and set the future date despite the long wait for us to see each other.

He will probably forget and move on, especially since we aren't exchanging messages in between our initial chat and that future fall date. When the day finally arrives, I go to see Mr. Honest in the morning, assuming my date with Mr. NFL will fizzle. I hit the road after sending Mr. NFL a note to confirm our plans–just in case. To my surprise, he answers and plans to come to my hotel that later that evening. He leaves his home late, and drives, unbeknownst to me, a full two hours to my hotel, arriving well after the suggested time of 10 pm. He is absolutely stunning to look at. Like most of my matches, the initial appeal is aesthetic. I see each one of these incredibly handsome, sexy young men as a gift to myself, allowing myself to enjoy the experience of being the object of their desire, if only for the moment. They're grateful for it.

He is recently retired from professional football, with a recognizable name, and he is beautiful – tall, muscular, dark, handsome – with a brilliant mind, everything I want. It is the first time I link twice in one day. It is not the last time or only time this happens, foreshadowing a chaotic revolving door of matches that happens over the coming winter. He is a spectacular lover who refuses cuddles afterwards, standing nearly nude, wearing nothing but crew high socks, in the full-length hotel window as he tells me it's not his style. He walks over to the bed and lounges himself out next to me, though.

We talk for a while before he rekindles the heat for one more round. He tucks me into bed and shows himself out, leaving the condom wrapper on the TV stand to be found by my breakfast date the next morning. Disappointingly, we never get to reconnect, even with the exchange of occasional messages on Instagram and SnapChat, and more than a few random incoming phone calls. He has a girlfriend for a short time, deletes his social media, but still calls me occasionally just to chat, always without warning and often without a clear purpose. Every so often, he reactivates his Instagram, but never for more than a couple of days, and he doesn't respond when I reach out, so I never see him again.

That breakfast date who finds the errant Magnum wrapper the next morning – Mr. Surfer – is a whole different type of match. He's been hanging around for far too long, a well-known red flag by this time, and he's utterly persistent in wanting to see me. He's found my Snapchat and Instagram, he has my phone number which I rarely give out, he won't stop asking to see me. Finally, I agree he can caddy a disc golf round for me. My date with Mr. NFL is coordinated with this event, too, but I tacitly agreed to allow Mr. Surfer to meet up with me based on the low expectations I have going into the weekend. After all, Mr. NFL and I made this plan months ago.

So, there I sit with two confirmed dates in my hotel after seeing Mr. Honest in the morning before check-in. It takes coordination, but I space them out. I have to convince Mr. Surfer that he can't come by the night before since I arrive late and need my rest. He is inquisitive and anxious when he shows up, admitting he doesn't want to have sex for fear of contracting a sexually transmitted disease. He assumes the number of partners I have is high enough for the risk to be real. He sees the Magnum wrapper next to the television and asks about it; I shrug it off and dismiss its presence. I assure him I get tested regularly and always use protection, but I don't really want to have sex with him anyway.

He's just as weird and awkward as I expect him to be and looks nothing like his photos, which show him boating, golfing, and surfing. He still pulls out a condom and tries anyway. It's unsatisfying, to say the least, and we stop after a few seconds since he can't keep an erection. Neither of us are really into it and I have somewhere to go so we hurriedly shower and dress. I check out of the room and head to the disc golf course after sending him the address.

Astonishingly, he actually shows up and carries my bag all day after the weirdly abrupt end to our encounter in the hotel room. I expected him to duck out and head home, never to be seen again. He pesters me for months afterwards to finish what we started, but I have no plans to be back in that area any time soon. I certainly don't travel just to link with someone who isn't all that appealing. He offers to come to me but refuses to go on a date or do anything other than link, so I ignore him. My inbox is full of unanswered messages as I grey rock him with icy cold silence until he moves on. It takes at least a year, and even then, he messages me periodically just to see if I have changed my mind. I never reply.

❖❖❖❖❖

Mr. Sunday and Mr. Massage show up in my life at the same time, in the late fall of 2020, maddening in their occupation of my time, usually with their absence and claims that they are on their way. They are among the regulars in the fall and winter months leading into 2021. Sometimes, Mr. Sunday is so unaware of time he shows up on Monday. A fantastic lover, tall, naturally lean, incredibly handsome, intellectual, and sweet but poorly educated. He is completely unaccountable and fails to live up to his full potential as an adult.

He barely works, usually third-shift manufacturing jobs that he doesn't take seriously and comes from a totally different world where careers and salaries are an abstraction. I am a consultant for an IT firm with a remote position, home office, and matching 401K; he's an occasional employee working for low wages with long periods of unemployment. It's challenging to avoid being classist. I'm not necessarily looking for a life partner to plan retirement with, but perhaps someone I can spend more meaningful time with. A travel partner for tropical beach vacations is a goal, so long as they can carry their own weight.

I dislike the waiting around though, and I especially dislike being up later than I intend. I catch myself thinking that Mr. Massage could have come and gone already, while wondering if Mr. Sunday will show up at all. It is usually worth it, though. He doesn't have other lovers and doesn't care that I do. He always offers full-service massages with happy endings, and never expects me to reciprocate in any way. It is delicious, and the sex that follows is hedonistic and consumptive. I can always smell him on my quilt for days afterwards which makes me wonder if my other lovers can, too. He says he will do anything for me, but he can't bring himself to be on time so after six months, our situation has mostly run its course. Aside from occasional messages to check if my temperature has warmed towards him, I only see him once more.

Mr. Massage, on the other hand, always offers a massage, which is his profession, but rarely comes through with more than a few minutes of light stroking before turning to the purpose of his visits. Sometimes we discuss traveling together, and dating like a couple, while we lay in bed afterwards, but then he always does this odd thing. Claiming he left something in his car, perhaps a gift of some sort, he tells me he will be right back. He leaves and does not return – for weeks. Even as he texts me that he's coming back soon, in a few minutes, I know he's already gone. He tells me, always from his car, that he needs to run for food, or meet a friend to loan them money, or just has to run a quick errand and leaves me lying in bed waiting for a return that never happens. He is short, fair complected, and handsome, with a smooth voice that coos all the right words into my ear while we climax together, and then he evaporates into the night leaving the cool silence of my irritation behind.

Nonetheless, I ask him to come back frequently over the course of 12 months for the sheer joy of his infatuated, but wholly contrived, lovemaking. He is in the shower in the basement bathroom of the master suite of my new house, having come directly from work, while I am at my desk getting divorced via Zoom on a warm fall afternoon at the end of November 2020.

I'm overlooking my massive private yard through the picture window in what used to be a dining room while I listen to the judge outline the terms of the divorce.

We are in my bed immediately afterwards and he evaporates instantly when he's finished. I return to my desk and see his car disappear behind the trees that line my long, winding, private driveway. It opens like a portal to a different world as it rises to meet the main road at the top of the hill, and he's gone. The last time I see him, he appears ragged and worn. I am shocked at the change from the days when he shows up in designer clothes and expensive sneakers. He asks to see me and requests I bring him something to eat if there are leftovers in my fridge, which I bring to a shady apartment complex.

While I wait in the parking lot, I see open-air drug dealing and probably prostitution. He doesn't want me to see where he's staying so he asked me to stay outside. It's probably a trap house. He hasn't been working and it looks like he is using drugs. From the passenger seat, he asks for money to go with the Tupperware container of soup and fresh baked biscuits I brought for him. I decline the request and tell him to keep the containers when he's finished. I never see him again, and when future matches give me an address in that complex, I block them without explanation. It's not a safe place.

Swiping right on disc golfers seems safe, and I do this periodically as I cultivate my regular rosters over the course of this story. It leads to a few awkward rounds, a few links of varying quality, and a couple of new, desperately needed friends in the disc golf community. But the very best disc golf encounter comes when I swipe right on the Cart Guy. He instantly chats me up about disc golf and mentions that we are already friends on Facebook, so I invite him to chat me up in messenger instead of Tinder.

The conversation is weird from the beginning and he's acting like we went from match to married when we move away from the Tinder platform. I try to cool off the banter and put off meeting him by letting him know I am busy all afternoon with planned disc golf rounds. I don't tell him that I'm playing with a Tinder match I saw at sunrise since that's not really his business. Somehow, he figures out which course and what time and he shows up first, introduces himself to the card as my date. He proceeds to play two rounds with me and the Tinder date I just spent the morning with, along with a couple of our mutual friends. The existing Tinder date, Short Guy, is already one of my regular encounters, and he is an incredibly good sport about being on an unannounced, unplanned double Tinder disc golf date.

We make it as awkward as possible with juvenile jokes about salted nuts, bad Tinder date stories, and general debauchery; everyone, including Cart Guy has a fantastic time. He chain-smokes cigarettes the entire time and when I duck out afterwards, I tell him I never date men who smoke so we can't date. He takes the dismissal well and we end up playing a lot more disc golf together over the next few years. He never realizes Short Guy is also a Tinder link, or that he basically crashed a pre-existing Tinder date. A year and a half later, Cart Guy is living in a tent at a campground with the love of his life, who is definitely the second woman he's dated since we met. Short Guy is still short, sexy, and available for fantastic links and occasional disc golf rounds. He is the first real "friends with benefits" connection that endures in equal parts friendship and benefits. Most of my connections, even the very best ones, end up lopsided. Usually on the benefits end and lacking in the true measures of friendship, but in some cases, like Sir V, it's the other way around.

Let's back up to when I find the Gold Standard, also known as Number One–his story parallels these events from the beginning and continues to this day. It is late October 2020 and I just moved into my new house; he's the first link I see here and embarrassingly, my mattress is still on the floor in my basement bedroom. He is the most beautiful man I have ever seen–the very definition of *glossy*. His profile has to be fake. It shows him wearing a suit, decked out in tens of thousands of dollars in diamonds, posing with a nice car, looking like a model with dreamy eyes, high cheekbones, and more of a snarl than a smile. I swipe right all the same, hot with desire I know will be unrequited from the start. To my surprise, it is an instant match, and he messages me first, within minutes, cutting to the chase to ask when he can see me.

I find a time in my schedule. An easier task in my new house where I am alone every other week. He arrives promptly, navigating his jet-black Nissan down my long winding driveway to park in front of my garage. He is wearing a suit and he's every bit as handsome as his profile suggests. I'm breathless with anticipation as I watch him from where I stand in the long sunroom that connects the garage to the rest of the house.

He steps out of his car, walks up to my door, and shyly introduces himself as he steps inside. He wastes no time grabbing me at the waist and kissing me. I turn to lead him to my bedroom, trailing my hand behind me with our fingers interlaced. He follows me through the kitchen and living room, down the hall, and into the basement where he proceeds to pin me up against the glass door of my walkout bedroom. Before I know it, he has me down on the mattress working me from behind, pressing me flat to the bed, with one strong hand grasping my throat, his body pressing against me. I can feel his warm, fast breath on the back of my neck as he finishes. He collapses on the bed next to me breathless and lays there a minute before getting up.

He cleans up some, using soap and a hand towel to carefully wash between his legs, paying close attention to the tip even though we used protection. Like a few of the stunning, young men before him, I presume I will never see him again so I savor our link as if it's the only time I will ever have him. He redresses in his suit, and leaves with that same shy grin and request that I not forget about him. I giggle because I think he will be the one to forget about me. From this moment on, he is the Gold Standard to which all suitors are compared, eclipsing The Best only in his desire to see me again, repeatedly. I was wrong about seeing him again.

He asks to come by again two days later, and I welcome him to my new home for another encounter. Each time thereafter, I savor our lovemaking like it will be our last time together. A few days after our first couple of links, I arrange for him to come by to do erotic massages for me and a girlfriend. She goes first. He brings her to heightened ecstasy while I watch from my bed which is now up on its frame. My massage is similar but ends with passionate lovemaking after my friend shows herself out early in my session. Eventually I tell him he is the Gold Standard and that he's the sexiest man alive – a mantra I repeat to him often. I tell anyone who asks that the Gold Standard knows he's him and everyone else knows they're not. Their collective feelings about this are irrelevant. Number One and I discuss dating more seriously, in public, despite our age gap, but decide against it when we consider our respective realities in our personal journeys. I'm not precisely sure what's going on in his life, but I'll soon find out.

Later that month while visiting me in my city, my mother uses the Gold Standard's massage services–not of the erotic variety. She grows envious of the quality of our connection. A widow for more than a year, and more than 70 years old, she's lonely and wants to find someone for the sunset years of her life. She signs up for her own Tinder account when she returns to her home two hours away in the remote, northern part of our state. Her contributions to this story are forthcoming, and brilliant, if not somewhat sad and hopeless.

After a few months of frequent links, of exceptionally high quality, during which we break the bed frame, I invite the Gold Standard to join me at a swinger's party. It's a group I spent time with when I was married which led to a close friendship with the co-hosts, and VIP guest status at most events. The first event we attend is a bar takeover with close to 75 guests. It is a spectacular time, and everyone loves him. As part of his introduction to my good friends and party cohosts, they look at me and ask, "what number is he" to which I immediately reply, "Number One, of course." This becomes another one of his nicknames, and we get more hysterical looks of surprise when he reveals his age, which by then is 27. Everyone knows I am older than 40 but he seems to have forgotten since he leans over and whispers to me "how old are you, anyway?" And I tell him with a smirk that I just turned 44—the same age as his mom—he's surprised but not turned off by the difference between us.

For the first time, at this party, the Gold Standard adds me to his social media feeds, as he seeks to be connected to the swinger's club Facebook page. It is my first peek into his real life. We stay out until sunrise on that icy cold winter night, retiring to our respective homes just after 4am. Later that morning when I open Facebook, I am greeted by an exaltation. There he is, Number One, glorifying the mother of his daughters, who is pregnant again, this time with his son – his King, his legacy. A brief scroll through her timeline shows they are affianced.

He moved to my community to be with her and his girls, one of whom is an infant in, October of 2020, just a few days before our first meeting. Despite frequent strife between them–she is often more babymama than fiancé–he really loves her, and it shows.

He is a good communicator. We already discussed more openly dating and decided against it, and now I know why. I press him: did he intend to marry her? Is that why he doesn't want to date openly? Is she aware of our connection? Does she know about the other lovers I know he has, or the parties we are going to? The answers are vague, but he leaves me convinced he is operating within the confines of their relationship agreement. I tell him I never want to be the reason his sweet little family doesn't work out.

Over the course of two years, we grow close and then apart, then close–almost declaring love for each other. Then, one day in May 2022, without warning, his social media is filled with their nuptials. A huge white wedding for which no expense is spared. I think back to all the savoring of our encounters. Memories designed to steel me for this moment when I know it's over between us. They are a welcome salve to my heartache and bring forth joy. I am equally crushed as I am relieved that he finally found his way to manhood with his wife and children.

Now, we profess our love to each other–it's genuine real affection and appreciation of the time we were able to share. Our connection is unbreakable, though, and he eventually shows up back on Snapchat with a new profile, and back in my new house for one last hurrah before I sell it and move out of town in late 2022. When I visit town to see my kids, we always find time to link and love on each other, in private of course, because he never really wanted me for more than the benefits anyway.

❖❖❖❖❖

Of course, there are other matches and links mixed into the evolution from invisible to visible. Most unworthy of remembering, their contact information lost to the chaos of eruptive inboxes–text messages, messenger, Snapchat, Instagram–a nonstop influx of photos, usually dick pics, chatter, and occasional requests for actual dates. Alongside a few minor connections that seem as if they'll gain traction, but they run their course quickly, and ebb off without fanfare.

Still, there are a few lovely connections that evolve. There is a doctor in the next town over who really wants a no-strings arrangement without anything more but is unsure of making the one-hour drive on the chance I am not anything like my profile. We arrange to video chat and he's convinced that I'm who I say I am, that I look like my photos, and that I'll be respectful of his need for space. We set a date and he comes to my house. He's skillful and adoring for that brief period we are together. The next time, I drive to him. We exchange a few visits, with interspersed casual chats to check in with each other, and assurances to meet again soon. I reach out for a date after a few months to learn he's moved to the east coast for work. Every so often, we still exchange a text message or two, just to remind ourselves of what we had, ever so briefly.

There is also a doctoral candidate at the university who I meet in his campus apartment on a hot fall night. He's lovely and lonely, far away from his home and family in Nigeria, with wildly aspirational goals to help and support the people of Africa through the application of health technology. He wants to give a voice to Black and African doctors whose work contributes to global public health discourse, both historically and in the present. I'm interested in all things academic, and we talk about his research, alongside other topics in the academy when we lay in bed afterwards. His current challenges are writings related to his dissertation which are due soon and he's struggling to make sure the words are translating correctly. I offer to read and edit his work; confident my professional skills will benefit his final submissions.

His writing is thoughtful and well documented, with little need for edits in the beginning. I can tell when he gets tired based on changes to the syntax that start showing up later in the documents. Along with offering minor edits, I suggest he start his next writing session mid-paper so he can use his fresh mind on the end instead of the beginning. Advice I should probably take myself as this manuscript grows from an idea into a novel.

He tells me he feels seen and heard when we are together, and even more so when he receives my edits and suggestions. He feels so comfortable, so good, so cared for–he is homesick. It's nice to have someone to care for in this way and he's deeply appreciative. He's shy about sex and the things he wants to do. He's never been able to explore his sexuality or desires with anyone before. Even when he takes me from behind, a relatively common and popular position, it's new for him to be allowed such latitude with a woman. He asks to see me again and if he can try other positions with me next time. Of course, I agree. He has no idea how free I am with my lovers, though he knows I have many. We have a few lovely, casual encounters before he must travel back to Africa to conduct primary research for his dissertation. When he returns to the US, our schedules don't align, and we always find ourselves in different states, sending each other updates about our lives and our work. Never reconnecting but also, never forgetting each other.

CHAPTER 4

SPINNING WHEELS

Despite a few lasting connections from the first Tinder profile, and a few lovely shorter encounters, I find myself spinning my wheels, unhappy and unfulfilled, and seeking validation in the form of new connections on Tinder. A new profile emerges in early 2021, with the same icy tag line–*feelings are gross; don't catch them with me*–followed by the qualifiers mentioned earlier on. I resume swiping, mostly left, in a false and hopeless search for a primary partner other than myself. Even through all the solopoly talk, I keep looking for that man. The one. The one who's glossy like the Gold Standard, a skilled lover like the Best, and completely enamored with me, nearly obsessed, like I am with myself.

I meet Mr. LDS and he gives off this air of interest that comes close. He's handsome, short, and muscular, with a lovely smile. He's an immigrant from Côte d'Ivoire who speaks French as well as English, and several other languages common in his homeland. He always showers me with compliments, which I ask for in French, and he obliges. Occasionally, he offers criticism (which I can do without) for making him leave my house the first night we met. It is the only time I have to actually ask someone to leave because he isn't taking the hint and he assumes he can stay the night since we are in bed together already.

He never really fully performs, finding it difficult to maintain an erection, and eventually finishes weakly on my belly. When he gets up to use the bathroom, I open the bedroom door to let my dog into the room, and get myself dressed to go upstairs, and in so doing escort my guest out the door. He is shocked it isn't a sleepover and later learns I have a disappointingly strict "no one spends the night" policy. Throughout our ongoing connection afterwards he offers suggestions on how he may want to make love to me while we sip coffee at the kitchen table. Sometimes, I take him downstairs to my bedroom, but he always falls short with performance anxiety and he remains flummoxed by the idea of having to leave afterwards.

He is wrought with guilt from his strict religious upbringing in contrast to his desire for sexual freedom which cultivates conflict with the Christian teachings of monogamy he grew up with. We never really seal the deal as each time we attempt to link, he is unable to sustain an erection. Still, we continue to chat, and he comes by for coffee and joints early on cold winter mornings when the kids aren't home. We talk about our matches and links, his numerous girlfriends named Jessica who challenge him in the most unique ways. We also discuss my own type, which is probably my problem. I match with men half my age, with amazing bodies, who often also have girlfriends and wives. Or have terrible personalities. Or are grossly irresponsible. But they are beautiful, and eager to meet me as long as I don't want to go on a date. In the beginning, I didn't really want dates, but as I settle into life after divorce, my needs change.

He tells me how amazing it would be if we could be together as a couple, which is something I don't want with him, and he knows it. Eventually, he cuts me off and moves on. Only after he tells me he's doing so and why. Still, he's one who resurfaces often over the next two years, running laps in my inbox, another huge red flag I acknowledge but sometimes still ignore.

A planned Arizona disc golf road trip in the spring of 2021 to celebrate my birthday brings concern from my mother. She begs me to bring someone along as if I am a teenager who will certainly be abducted if I travel alone. There are several new matches, including one man who happens to own property in Arizona. Despite the fact that I only sort of like him after a few brief and unusual meetings, and the part where I don't really think I need a travel partner, I make the offer and he accepts. He promises to have cash to contribute, agrees to play disc golf along the way, and wants to explore the idea of going all the way to L.A. to see the beach, returning through Las Vegas, and making more of an adventure of the trip. I love the ocean and roadtrip adventures have always held appeal, so I agree.

It turns into a shitshow of epic proportions. To begin with, he is more or less broke and promises that he gets paid a few days into the trip but doesn't tell me until we are already one state away from home. We drive through the night towards Denver, despite my suggestion that we do not do that. Arriving in Denver at 6 am is not the move; but he ends up doing exactly that while I sleep through most of Nebraska. He pulls into a rest stop just outside of Denver for some shuteye about 3:30 am and asks to switch seats so he can rest on the passenger side.

We can see a hotel from the rest stop, and I suggest we check-in but he assures me that it is unnecessary. It's 4 am when we settle into uncomfortable car seats to rest. I am in the driver's seat, so at 5 am, I decide I need coffee and make the rest of the drive into Denver with a stop at Starbucks along the way. When we arrive in Denver, I pull into the breakfast spot we had agreed to earlier and shake him awake.

He refuses to go inside because of Covid. I am more than a little miffed. It's my actual birthday and we are in Denver at 6 am, despite my request not to push through the night, and now this man doesn't even want to go inside to eat. He also begins complaining about the discomfort he's experiencing from sleeping in the car, which I cited as a good reason not to drive through the night in the first place, and the main argument for checking into that hotel we saw from the rest stop. Ugh. This might have been a bad decision. I briefly entertain the notion of bringing him directly to the airport.

Instead, I decide to drive us over to the hotel I have booked for the night of my birthday to see about a possible early check-in. Even though it's only 9 am on a Saturday, the desk agent is able to get me in a room. We go inside and sleep like the dead for a few hours, have some reasonably good sex that doesn't include any oral for me, despite his demand for a blowjob with every link. He doesn't do that, *ewwww*, which begs the question of why I even entertain him in the first place. Finally, after hot showers, we go do something I want to do for my birthday. We hike Dinosaur Ridge. It's an easy walk up and around the ridge on a paved road. The fossils and stratigraphy are, to me, as stunning as the view of Red Rock Amphitheater across the road. This is my favorite short, easy outdoor route in the area and clearly the most technical thing we can do, given the new, white loafers he's wearing.

For some reason, this man who agreed to disc golf with me along the way brought two new pairs of white loafers for the trip and no sandals or tennis shoes. Instead of a course, we end up at a pro shop where I get a recommendation for a good course in Pueblo, and I buy a few choice discs. The shop attendant recognizes my disc golf tattoo and when I tell him it's my birthday, he brings out a few nice discs he has stashed in the backroom. It's the closest thing to birthday gift.

We return to the hotel, and I discover he's not going into a restaurant for dinner either. It's still my birthday. I reconsider the airport but decide a walk downtown, some takeout, and a good night's sleep should improve my attitude. There is live music floating out from the bars and restaurants of downtown Denver. We still don't go inside. The cool spring air is refreshingly mixed with the disappointment and misgivings for having invited someone so lame along on my birthday vacation.

In the morning, we leave for my girlfriend's bed and breakfast in New Mexico without trying to see my sister's kids who still live in Denver. I message their dad before we leave home, and he doesn't reply so I don't follow up when I'm there. We opt for a less-traveled route through the mountains, and we are welcomed by my friend and her partner with open arms after a long, sunny drive along the High Road to Taos. They cook us dinner, and make fresh coffee for me, THC cocktails for everyone else.

The host and I are loosely coupled through a mutual friend, and we solidified our friendship through our shared interest in beadwork and minerals and crystals. We also share the unique experience of having left a terrible road trip partner on the side of the road thousands of miles from home. I did it to a woman when I was in my late teens in the summer of 1997 when she aggressively disrespected me at a stoplight. We took a roadtrip from northern Minnesota and I left her on a street corner in L.A. when I kicked her out of my car. I know she eventually made it home, but I don't know how. The bed and breakfast host did the same to a woman more recently when they traveled to a beadwork show and her travel partner became unbearable. Her drama played out on Facebook and the two of us bonded via messenger after she made a post about leaving her friend behind. I had to tell her I had done the same thing!

We reminisce about our road trip fails over dinner and laugh into the evening about how difficult it is to navigate the road with some people, her partner and mine listening and laughing and drinking. After driving all day, I retire to bed earlier than everyone else, and this is where the story gets weird.

I'm asleep almost instantly, so when he follows me to bed a little bit later, the ruckus wakes me up. He's tossing and turning, talking unintelligibly, and clearly too drunk. He wants something from me, not sex, but his desires are unclear. It takes close to five minutes of guessing games to figure out he wants to be the little spoon. Now, at 5-foot and four inches and about 140 pounds, I am not big spoon material. Particularly for a man who's approaching 6-feet and 200 pounds. Plus, I am already sleeping, or at least had been sleeping. It takes me scolding him like a small child to get him to shut up and go to sleep, and when he finally does, he begins to snore loudly.

I am now wide awake and remain so for hours. He smells awful, and this is when I realize that he isn't some irreverent, silly man who sometimes carries an odd, sweet aroma, which was my initial impression of him after our first few meetings. He's a drunk who hides his liquor in juice bottles and is constantly off-gassing scotch. How had I not noticed this sooner?

I wake up early with the intention of putting this weird encounter behind us. We have a long drive across New Mexico to reach Canyon de Chelly, our next destination, and later his property in Arizona, which is an open tract of land adjacent to the Petrified Forest National Park. I am committed to enjoy the day and the rest of my trip. He wakes up aggravated and tells me he would have slept better if he had been held properly in the night. I just ignore him and walk over to the kitchen to have coffee and breakfast with my friend before we leave. He follows behind me ten minutes later and acts like nothing unusual is happening.

When we hit the road, there's palpable tension simmering in the chilly mountain air. We head towards Arizona following the High Road to Taos down to Santa Fe before heading west on US 25. I am unsure when, but on one stop or another, his scotch bottle–previously stashed in the far back of my Outback–migrates to his lap in the front seat. It's just over three quarters full, and honestly, I don't feel like arguing, so he drinks while I drive. Eventually we have to start making frequent stops for him to pee and he spends the majority of the day talking about how Pisces, like me, are always scheming and usually just plain evil in their shrewd strategy towards coming out on top of every interaction. Quite the long compliment.

When we arrive at Canyon de Chelly, the overlooks are all unexpectedly closed as part of the pandemic response. Other National Parks and Monuments are open; however, this one is on the Navajo Reservation, whose sovereignty overrules and whose pandemic response is still in full effect. The tribe has not yet reopened the parks and public spaces in their jurisdiction. We drive down to the gate of one overlook and turn around, parking so he can look around a little, and pee again, of course.

A car pulls up and the locals inside encourage us to drive around the barrier like they have so we can see the overlook. I insist we don't have time and load him into the car to head for his property, which we want to see before dark. As we are driving, he convinces himself that *he* made a good decision to not follow the locals around the gate. I don't bother countering his narrative, but I know he is completely unaware of the nuanced dynamics at play. Skirting a closed boundary on a federal land is a bad idea under all circumstances, and this is no exception. He continues to drink as we cross the desert from Canyon de Chelly to the Petrified Forest National Park, reducing his bottle of scotch to the dregs and increasing his verbal diarrhea.

He is impressively drunk, and the sun is sinking low in the sky when we finally approach our destination there are numerous exits, stops, pee breaks, and turnarounds before we arrive in the correct place. We proceed into the desert on two ruts carved into the hardpan landscape to find his plot of land. The first stop is at the entry gate to the national park; it's closed and there's nothing but a parking lot and scrub brush. He gets out to pee and I look at the map to orient myself. When he gets back in the car, he explains that we need to head to the next exit to access his land. Following his directions, we get back on the highway and exit a mile further down the road, and he says it appears totally unfamiliar and everything looks different than he remembers from his last visit a year earlier. He recalls the low clearance tunnel that passes under the freeway, so we follow the road away from town. We cross into the desert, and I steer the car along the ruts as he tells me where to turn and we finally arrive at his land.

He walks around the plot, pausing to pee yet again, and despite the unfamiliar feeling he has about his property, he wants me to drive around on it in a show of ownership. Driving on the delicate desert landscape is something I would normally never do. It's his land though, so why not? He throws the empty scotch bottle out the window onto *his* property, asking me if we can stop at the liquor store later for more booze, and we leave. He wants to show me one more thing about his land before we move on towards Phoenix where I have friends and where I want to finally play a round of disc golf. Phoenix is home to the famous Fountain Hills disc golf course and I'm not going to miss out on the opportunity to play there.

We drive deeper into the high desert, he's struggling to make sense of the map and our geography relative to the national forest property to which his land is adjacent, and he realizes–that wasn't *his* land. Somehow, I am not surprised. The sun has set by now, so I navigate back to the highway in the dark where I find myself at the parking lot of the national forest again. I use my phone to book a nearby hotel room while gets out of the car to pee, again. We drive towards Flagstaff in silence at first, and then he's pontificating how it's "just like a white woman to leave a Black man on uncharted land."

He's clearly attempting to discharge his shame and embarrassment to create a narrative where he bears no responsibility for the errors–trespassing, littering, and driving off road on private property. Plus, he reminds me to take him to the liquor store since his scotch is gone. I invite him to continue, to get it all out, and then, at his request, I tell him what I really think: he's a drunk and he's evading responsibility for trespassing, littering, and the general misdirection by verbalizing all this nonsense rather than accept that he made some rather significant errors in judgement. He's appalled that I think him a drunk, it's an outrage! He's shouting–our conversation is over, our relationship is over (if we ever really had one), and don't forget to stop at the liquor store before we get to the hotel.

❖❖❖❖❖

The silence that follows burns hot in the air. I've been handling drunks since childhood so at this point, I know the silence is better than an ongoing argument. We arrive at the hotel, and I nearly forget the liquor store. He reminds me and seems to have forgotten why our ride was so quiet. He offers to get me something to drink, and I ask for water. He comes back with a case of Corona, vodka, and juice. I send him back in for water before we head to the hotel to check-in. He waits in the car. The family checking-in ahead of me is in obvious discourse. Three tentative, perhaps anxious teenagers who know exactly how bitterly angry their parents are, crowd the desk until they settle their room situation and head for the elevator. When it's my turn, I ask for two beds and I'm glad my travel partner is still in the car.

When we get to the room, we take turns going back and forth to the car. He goes down first to collect his belongings and bring them back to the room since his hands were full with his haul from the liquor store when we first come up to the room. He mentions the arguing parents he sees in the parking lot as I'm leaving to go down to the car myself. They are still there when I get downstairs and sit down in the driver's seat with a huge sigh of relief.

I use that time to call my mom who shrugs it all off like I have no options but to suck it up and carry on. I am barely listening to her while I listlessly watch the couple with their over articulated gestures that suggest they're on the brink of their own divorce. I hang up without giving my mom's advice any consideration and head back up to the room. He offers me a beer when I return and is surprised to learn that "I do not drink" means I don't even drink beer. Undeterred, he tries to join me in my bed and spills a full bottle of water on the bedside table. There's no way. Scoldingly, I order him to clean up the mess and send him to his own bed where he's asleep almost instantly, loudly, off gassing the sweet stench of scotch and juice. I shop flights to assess the cost to send him home. It is surprisingly affordable.

But I am also genuinely curious about his property, so the next morning I am packed, showered, and ready to go long before he wakes up. The plan is to take him to see his actual property, and then drive to Phoenix, where I'll leave him. I check the cost of flights again. They have gone up slightly. After I shun his advances–he put his unwashed crotch in my face seeking a blowjob at least, if not more, when he wakes up–and send him to the shower, we get in the car where the GPS coordinates listed on his deed are pre-programmed into the map.

We are sitting in the car in the hotel parking lot, getting ready to pull out, when I tell him he is never to drink in my car again. He's holding a styrofoam cup of hotel ice, and probably vodka, in which he pours his juice while he agrees to my request. The tension is again palpable, and he makes no attempts to shift the dynamic. The cup disappears quickly. I am still unsure where he disposed of it since I focus on the road and ignore him entirely on the 20-minute drive to his land. It was almost certainly alcohol.

The property is actually amazing. There is an unmatched view of the desert, and it actually *shares* a fence line with the Petrified Forest National Park. The land rolls away majestically towards the White Mountains. It is approximately two miles from the property where we trespassed the day before. It is situated so that it's entirely private without any houses or development in sight. No wonder the buildings and surroundings we could see from *his land* the day before seemed so unfamiliar. We stay on what constitutes a road in this part of the desert and park near the fence. I get out to walk around, surveying the land with awe and appreciation. He doesn't deserve this. And, I can do better.

When he's had his fill, we navigate back to the highway, and once we are heading west again, the words come tumbling out with familiar ease. "When we get to Phoenix, I am dropping you off and continuing without you." He stares at me in stunned silence, so I continue "this is my vacation, which I intend to enjoy, and so far, I have not enjoyed your contributions and do not believe I will enjoy any further interaction with you."

I'm prepared for this, but still somehow shocked when he tells me he doesn't have any money for anything if I leave him behind. I CashApp him $250 and tell him to figure it out before we get to Phoenix, or I will take him directly to the airport. He has two hours and it's a small price to pay to be rid of him. He books a hotel and asks if I can bring him with me when I head back home. I cannot.

On the drive to my friend's house, after dropping him off at the hotel, I decide to book the man a flight home. The cost is less than $150 on Frontier, but the itinerary is seven hours, so I check other providers, and by paying just a few extra dollars, I can get him on a Sun Country flight with a 23-hour itinerary and no checked bags. A much better fit for the situation. I book it for him and send him the details with an invitation to stop by my place when I'm home to collect whatever he has left in my car. It's $400 that, just like him, I never see again.

The rest of the road trip is amazing, though, and while in Phoenix, I finally connect with the Nigerian soccer player I've been flirting with for months. It's not clear how we initially matched on Tinder when he lives in Tennessee, and I am in the Midwest. Our connection transitions to Instagram and Snapchat, so as he moves around the country, from Tennessee to Arizona, we maintain contact in hopes of someday connecting. He comes to my room for an evening and devours me with the intensity of a professional athlete. We both hope for more, but that one hot Phoenix night is all we have together. His deep voice and heavy accent rumble in my mind for weeks afterwards, the sight of his crown between my thighs seared into my memory bank among the best of my lovers. In the morning, and every day I'm in Arizona, I disc golf a new course. I stop to play in Pueblo, Colorado on the way home at the course recommended to me on my birthday as the oldest course in Colorado and one of the first permanent courses in the US. It feels like success.

When I return home, I notice shattered glass all over my driveway, even though I made a call to ensure his vehicle would be open with the key inside when he returned. Mr. Arizona must have broken a window on his van. He proceeds to present the trip to Phoenix as an intentional business trip, with social media posts of him walking around downtown Phoenix and posting up under the palm trees. I want to make sure the true story is told. So, one last time, I link up with Mr. Sunday to tell him this tale. I know he's a cousin to the drunken mess I traveled with and will make sure at least his mama and his brothers know he was left behind for being a drunk. It's time to delete my Tinder profile and start over again.

The spring leads to more failed matches and terrible links on Tinder and an attempt at something different–Hinge and Bumble–which present me with nearly all the same profiles I see on Tinder with a few exceptions that turn into lovely connections and long-term partners–Mr. Bush and Osiris both come from Hinge. The first one is an invisible link, one who only wants to meet for sex and casual banter, to which I agree based solely on his appearance. He's physically stunning with rippling muscles shining through skin that's light and velvety soft from coco butter. He's always freshly showered when I see him, and he greets me at the door in athletic shorts. His photos on Instagram make him look huge but he's actually more my size, almost delicate and short, with incredible muscular definition that gives a false impression of bulk. We link periodically, sometimes frequently, for a year before the situationship runs its course. We still reach out to one another in hopes our schedules will align again. They don't and we stop linking. We leave the situation with nothing but good things to say about each other and our connection.

Osiris is not invisible. Like me, he's divorced with two kids, in his mid-forties, and he's absolutely stunning, with well-defined abs, and a lean, strong body from years of martial arts training. He speaks French, English, and several dialects from his home country of Togo. We meet at the botanical gardens, a favorite first date for me, since it's low pressure and totally free. Afterwards, we walk over to a local pizza shop to get slices and talk about the type of relationship and connection we are seeking. He's impressed with both locations and decides he'll visit again on his own time, with his kids, who are living with him for the summer. A few weeks later, we meet for dinner, and we link afterwards. It's amazing, so I invite him to join me at Opera in the Park later in the month.

We make plans and arrive at the park to find a spot on the lawn well in advance of the performance and I casually steer us away from my cousin when I see him to avoid an awkward encounter. My mother and auntie are on their way and will certainly sit with my cousin, or so I think, and when they arrive, they walk straight for us. My mom doesn't even see me at first but I am still mortified. As it turns out, the two of them and their friends had reserved seats earlier in the day, and the two of us randomly sat in the same spot, only inches away from their blankets on the lawn. So, Osiris, on our third date, meets my mom, two of her sisters, her brother and his husband, a small group of their friends, and my cousin who eventually wanders over to say hello.

During intermission, we find a dark, out-of-the-way place in the park to link quietly before casually returning to our seats to watch the second act with my family. After this, we ebb and flow, meeting up periodically to link, which always includes some casual banter about our dating adventures. He tells me he's banned from tinder, which has not yet happened to me.

We share occasional meals, he does a professional photoshoot for me, he learns massage (at which he excels) by practicing on me, and, of course, we have sex frequently (at which he also excels). He longs for a girlfriend and partner, partially so he can attend swinger parties, an inherently couples' activity where single women, but not usually single men, are welcome. Eventually, he finds his way into the Facebook swinger groups to which I belong, so perhaps someday we can partner up to attend an event, but for now, our connection grows into a genuine friendship, with benefits. He never pursues a partnership with me, though, which I appreciate since he's almost everything I want, but I know in my heart he is not everything I need.

When I leave town just over a year later, in distress, heading where the climate suits my clothes–Hawaii–he helps manage my home while it's for sale. He stops by to air it out and tidy up in advance of showings and checks in during the depths of winter to make sure the mechanicals are in good working order. The balance between friendship and benefits becomes uneven towards our friendship, and as the physical distance between us grows, our sexual connection cools off. It may not be over but it's definitely on hold.

Bumble lasts only one day. When I receive a screenshot of my profile in my Instagram inbox from a stranger, I delete my profile and the app. The suitor asks if it's me in the photo and says he clicked on an Instagram photo in my Bumble profile, and since I have my accounts linked, it brings him directly from Bumble to my Instagram page. I do not believe this is how the platform works, but unsure and totally sketched out, I immediately delete my profile on that site. It's one dating platform I never use again, even after being banned from Tinder a year later, I elect to use other platforms instead. The man on Instagram persists and says he's disappointed we didn't match when he swiped right, asking if we can chat anyway since we are both seeking dates. I block him, because no, that's not how any of this works. We didn't match and I am not interested, or I would have swiped right. Honestly, I'm not even sure if I ever saw his profile in the first place, and he is not my type even if we are both single.

CHAPTER 5

RECYCLING AND UPCYCLING

Before my connection with Osiris unfolds over the summer, it comes around to be Mother's Day in 2021. One year after I decide to divorce my husband, and at the very early stages of my connection to Osiris. The icy stillness of those words still hangs in the air around me, haunting me with all those Mother's Days that went uncelebrated, invisible, with kids too little to know any better or any different. I delete my Tinder profile yet again for an intentional hiatus, but that doesn't change the frequency of random links. Several of my established matches–the Gold Standard, Short Guy, Mr. Bush, Bubbles, Mr. LDS–come through on a regular basis when our schedules mesh, but there are no dates. Only links. Even Osiris becomes invisible opting for massage sessions rather than dinner plans, or cooking for me in his apartment, which he does with minimal skill. The lack of kitchen skills is yet another indication he's not a good option for a long-term partner anyway, so the shift in our relationship status is welcome.

It's around this time that I start receiving all sorts of random messages from all sorts of random men, most of whom I matched with on Tinder at some point. And, regardless of whether we have previously met in real life, there is a sudden and renewed interest in meeting me now. The messages come two or three a day, often more, every day for weeks at time, with occasional unexplained radio silences interspersed. They often start out with a brief greeting, to which I respond with a pair of question marks when I don't recognize incoming numbers. The responses vary–hurt, angry, resigned–to learn I have no idea who they are, even after they send their name. Without a photo, or some specific touchpoint to identify them, I can't place them. Names still mean nothing to me for those who haven't proven themselves worthy of an immediate meeting or repeat visit, which comes before saving their phone number in my contacts.

Sometimes the messages arrive anonymously via SMS/text, other times on social media platforms–Instagram, Snapchat, Facebook–where at least they are attached to a face and a name. There is always a request to link up, and more often than not, an unrequited declaration of their undying love for me. They need me. They can't live without me. They don't even know me, even if they have met me, and I don't know them. But they're insistent. They must have me.

How am I supposed to respond? More often than not, they are accompanied by an unsolicited dick pic or tribute video that shows them masturbating. Some of them I entertain. Most of them I do not.

There's a reason their numbers aren't saved in my phone, or that I had not seen them the first time around. There is also a reason I only saw them once and have not saved their number. Each time I give in to one of them, I remind myself, I can do better. They are terrible lovers, their houses are messy or they're homeless, they're unemployed–the list of reasons not to see them, or not see them again are countless. It always becomes immediately evident again whenever I agree to meet one of the men who sends me this type of random message.

On top of all this random traffic, from the very beginning of the divorce process, I have been adding handsome men to my Facebook profile from the "People You May Know" offerings like it *was* Tinder. During this time, many of these men begin to notice me. They show up in my inbox wondering how and why we are connected in the socials, and many of the local connections become links–a librarian, a college football player whose an NFL recruit, a Muslim man who stops by after dark during Ramadan, a young former military man I occasionally bump into on the disc golf course. Like all the others, they are young, Black, and absolutely stunning, aesthetic little gifts to myself. I savor them and their desire like fine wine, swirling them in my mind, breathing their essence, gently tasting them on my lips with a quivering tongue. They're happily enthusiastic for an opportunity to bed an older white woman. The age dynamic at play is almost always discussed, and I learn the contrasting skin tones are part of the appeal to both myself and my partners. We like what we like.

The first time I link with someone random from Facebook is late 2020, just after I move into the new house. He owns a series of rental properties in a nearby town, which is important to this story, because the entire time we are chatting, I tell him I can't see him due to the work involved with changing a light fixture in my new home. Insisting it's easy enough, he convinces me to carve out some time for him, and he drives the two hours to my house. Just as attractive as his photos, with long healthy, thick dreads, dark black skin, he is broad and muscular, with a deep voice. It turns out he's Jamaican. We chat briefly while I give him the long and winding tour through my house to the basement bedroom. He sees the light fixture project as soon as he walks in the house and comments how he "does that kind of thing all the time" in the context of the rental properties he owns and manages.

In the bedroom, he's creative and active, with an approach that border on domination, asking me to take submissive postures that give him control over my whole body. I enthusiastically agree. He has decent stamina, and we move through multiple orgasmic placements. Against the closet door, pinned in the doorway, folded over the bed, on my knees in the walkway, we make full use of my entire bedroom suite. Twenty minutes later, he tells me he gets too nervous being away from home for too long and he has to leave. He walks past the lighting project, which does in fact turn out to be rather quick and easy. He wishes me good luck with the installation on his way out the door.

It isn't long before he's asking to see me again and I politely decline without offering an explanation, but he's persistent so I see him one more time with similar results. The sex is amazing, but he can't stay. He's too nervous when he's this far from home, a trait I come to detest among suitors. How am I supposed to date someone who can't leave the house without having a panic attack when I always want to be out doing something? He compliments my new light fixture on his way out the door this time.

We are connected on Facebook and one day, after a little friendly banter under one of his posts, a strange woman shows up in my inbox wanting to argue with me about him. She changes her mind and unsends the message while I'm reading it and blocks me but it's clear she thinks they're together. With absolutely zero interest in the drama that always seems to find me, I block him rather than confront him. He finds me on Instagram to ask why and I let him know I don't appreciate his girlfriend showing up in my inbox, nor did I particularly appreciate his support with my light fixture. Then I block him from Instagram, too. He finds me on Snapchat and apologizes profusely for the drama and begs to see me again. I block him there, too. He makes new profiles periodically over the course of the next year in an ongoing but ultimately unsuccessful attempt to see me again.

The librarian is an oddity for me though, overweight and out of shape, he's in his mid-40s like me, and educated. The sex is only ok, though. He thinks it is way better than I do and feels like we have an intense connection. I am actually optimistic about him at first, thinking I can see myself in a relationship with a professional my own age, even if the sex leaves something to be desired. But then I come to learn that he lives with a roommate in a terrible apartment complex, and we cannot go on dates. He is too anxious to leave the house for a social outing–no dinners, no operas, no concerts, nothing. But I can come over and have sex with him whenever I want because he does enjoy that. Sir, that's going to be a hard no. To this day, he keeps trying to get my attention for another link as long as it doesn't involve a date.

We try a casual outing, a trip to Costco, but even this is more than he can bear to be in public, so after several attempts at arranging actual dates with him, I just stop answering his messages. I don't need nonstop elaborate dates with a partner, but I do want to be able to enjoy the cultural offerings in our city, which are frequent and amazing, without having to coerce my partner to leave the house. Plus, I am in no hurry to settle for someone who doesn't meet the full spectrum of my needs. He's a nice man, though, so I almost feel bad about wanting to be friends with him since he's not receptive to the idea that our connection isn't what he thinks it is.

The college football player and NFL recruit is 22, almost too young, but he's grown and oh so handsome. The bar is set on the lower age range with him, though. One must be at least 22 years of age to board this ride. It isn't until we have linked once and tried several times to connect again, without success, that I realize he has a baby on the way with the love of his life. Like the Gold Standard, he is affianced and I'm more of a trophy to him. They're a stunning couple and so well-loved by their families, which I can see in their Facebook feed. The baby is adorable, and this man is still trying to darken my doorway, so I ask him about his relationship. He loves her dearly, but she can't tolerate his unusually large size more than once a week, sometimes less, and his sex drive is much higher than she will accommodate. She's also vanilla, and he's looking for a more adventurous lover and knows from experience I'll meet his expectations. I put him off, unconvinced that she's aware and approves of his extracurricular activities, but we continue to chat and talk about the types of things we might want to do with each other–all of it pure fetish-based fantasies. He wants to orchestrate a gang bang.

Like many young men, he's interested in having sex with older women, and like many young Black men, he's attracted to older white women. As much as these young Black men are gifts to myself, I am also the fetish they didn't know they needed. Never their romantic interest, only their fantasy, and sometimes, like with this one, I am their sneaky link. I start to feel like a professional side piece.

On Facebook, I am friends with his older brother, also a married family man, and the Librarian is shocked to think that the older of them is one of my links. He is not, but I appreciate the confidence of the assumption. He too is a stunning specimen of a man, but he's not in my inbox like his little brother. I don't mention my actual link with the younger brother since it's never been my intention to knowingly be the other woman, and I don't want to ruin a good thing by airing that encounter, even in privacy.

Mohammed–the most common name in the world and therefore the only real name in the book–is a stunning, tall, thin, dark fashionista from West Africa. He has a full head of hair, thick beard, and a thoughtful arrogance about him. The first time he visits, it's under the guise of going for a walk, but he really wants to walk me across the expanse of my lawn, through the rooms of my house, and into to my basement bedroom where he can lay me down me down for his pleasure, which is exactly what I want. And exactly what ends up happening. He comes by semi frequently during the month of Ramadan, after working the late shift at his second job. It is often way too late in the night for me, but it's after he's broken his daily fast and before sunrise. I would give anything to shift that casual encounter into an intentional relationship with this man. He's stylish, thoughtful, introspective, and professional in his demeanor–everything I think I want in a partner. He likes to lay in bed and discuss current issues between lovemaking and before disappearing into the night. When Ramadan ends, he disappears entirely.

It's during this time–late spring 2021–when a brief conversation with a former professional colleague and sometimes professional collaborator turns sexual. "We're both grown," he says to me when he invites me to his apartment for an evening of casual lovemaking.

I lay in his bed afterwards and watch him iron his suit for the next day. I think about how nice it would be to find a partner like him. Grown, career-oriented, organized, driven, motivated, and disciplined. It is incredibly sexy. He's lovely, athletic, and smart–both educated and intelligent. He becomes a somewhat regular lover over the course of the next two years. We discuss going on proper dates and attending events together, but when the time comes, he's never available. He likes me, but he doesn't "like me–like me" with the casual obsession I would want from a partner.

I am beginning to miss having a partner, so that thought begins melting the icy cool façade that's been keeping my matches and links from becoming anything more serious. Mr. "We Grown" and I continue to link occasionally, and the topic of going on actual dates resurfaces but never materializes. We maintain our professional connection but the sexual connection fades when I move out of town the following year.

As a woman who loves disc golf, perhaps it makes sense to match up with and date disc golfers, but I also have a strong preference for Black men, which are few and far between on the disc golf course, so the opportunity to date Black disc golfers is rare. The Short Guy is an awesome good time on the course, a rare intersection between my type and my favorite activity, but he's not really a smart match for dating. He drinks and parties way more than I do, so we remain friendly, sometimes with incredible benefits, and I move on to cultivate other matches even while we continue to link frequently.

A random Facebook connection reaches out to play disc golf with me–his name is Bubbles and he's young, handsome, Black, and homeless, which I find out only after we have met up, played a few rounds, and linked a few times. He's bouncing between girlfriends. He always keeps one gal on the side, and he wants me to be his second option, but he also expects me to minimize or eliminate links with other men. His main girl is at home after she quit her job, sold her car, and commits to taking care of him and his household, which is really just her apartment. He's not sure if this is what he wants so he's been sleeping in his car but reconsiders when he learns that I don't let men spend the night. He moves in with her, fights for custody of his son, who he has with another woman, and he gets his current girlfriend pregnant. She decides against having a baby with him, but they remain committed to cultivating a "traditional" family with a working dad and stay-at-home mom.

Despite his messy circumstances we continue to link occasionally, and like many of the men with messy lives, he's so very good in bed and incapable of truly meeting my needs outside of that domain. He's fit and handsome, his dark skin always smooth and warm, his grin charms everyone he meets, and he measures well above average which is always my preference. He lasts just long enough, he likes to move through positions, provides oral stimulation without hesitation, and goes a second time, and third time.

He can be quick to sneak in a stealthy link on the course or take his time when we are uninterrupted in my bedroom where his insecurity sometimes shows. He's self-deprecating in a way that suggests he's aware of his shortcomings. He doesn't mind occasionally mowing my lawn or moving heavy items around the house and sometimes likes to come over just to visit.

Often, he talks about how he wants me to be one of his exclusive side pieces, and how he's frustrated that I belong to me and not to him and take more partners than he's comfortable with. Yet, he still asks to come over, to link, to act like we are in love, but like all the others, after the first few times doing something (e.g., disc golf) he only calls when he wants sex. Aside from all his other red flags, this is a common thread with my online matches–they might take me on one or two dates, but they just want access to my bedroom without having to be seen more than absolutely necessary–*invisibility*.

The best match from this time comes in the fall of 2021–the Man from Atlanta. He's one of those random Facebook adds, with long dreads, a lean physique, and a carefully curated newsfeed comprised of financial advice, entrepreneurship content, and promotion of his various brands. It isn't until he leaves that I google him and realized who he really is. It has never occurred to me that I should look at his, or anyone else's, online presence aside from their Facebook profiles. All I know is that I send him a single emoji–a pink and purple fairy–and he is mine. A simple trick employed over and over again, with the most handsome men on my timeline that always leads to at least a good conversation and often what amounts to a long-distance sexualized friendship, which I appreciate. Sometimes, though, it results in much more.

This is one of those times. The Man from Atlanta books a flight and a room and sends me money to get my nails done. He comes to my city so he can spend a weekend playing out his teacher fantasies with me. We talk about his desires and fantasies around dominating white women over the course of the week before he arrives and, with my enthusiastic consent, we play out every one of his youthful dreams. Including a long-term financial arrangement where I send him a portion of the unsolicited gifts I receive from strangers on the internet (a surprisingly common occurrence in the CashApp era). And at his insistence, I start making monthly deposits into my own investment account, which he advises, but of which I retain complete control, to build my own wealth portfolio.

Before any of that, though, the Man from Atlanta flies into the local airport where I pick him up. We stop at the grocery co-op to grab some organic fruits, vegetables, and snacks on the way to my house. From the moment we walk in the door, we are disrobed, and intensely involved in playing out his dominating teacher fantasies. All weekend we have sex like teenagers–over and over again–sometimes finishing with an intense blowjob, others, in extremely dominant positioning. I have no option but to take it all from him. Once he even finishes on my face, with the glasses on, upon his request.

I cook a vegan meal of bruschetta tomatoes and bread for him while he naps on my couch. We talk about the rest of our lives over dinner. He tells me he is married, but separated, and wants to have Black children someday, but also wants me to submit to him like a concubine in a fin-dom style relationship. It's a possibility as long as he can accept that I'm solopoly, so we can cultivate this dynamic to our mutual agreement, as long as he knows he's not the only one to whom I relate. He is mature beyond his 31 years and his ambition is admirable. He is writing a book, and already the CEO of two firms, so I am able to provide professional writing support for his many ventures, too, beyond the cash gifts, since writing is what I do. He is delicious and desirable, and he's famous. The google results reveal that he's well-known and well-regarded fintrepreneur. He laughs when I tell him I had not done this in advance, and he suggests I wait to google him until after he leaves, and further insists a man without at least some google results is probably beneath me. My own google results are half the reason he responds to me in the first place. A simple search on my name reveals my professional presence which, for the right man stimulates interest, after all, I am a professional in the IT-sector.

This experience is transformative as it is the first, but not the last time a man boards a plane and books a room to meet me in real life. He ups the ante on the type and quality of men that I believe are possible as partners, even when I more frequently and continually meet unworthy and all too often, homeless men. He has me saving for my future, investing in him and his brand, generating returns that keep giving, and importantly, he encourages me to seek more genuine connections with high quality men. And he orders me to define what quality means to me–to articulate what I want and settle for nothing less. We continue to look for those reconnection points where we can pick up our physical relationship even after more than a year has passed. I know I will see him again, it's just a matter of when and where.

CHAPTER 6

RETURNS

It's September 2021 when conditions of the pandemic permit work travel again, and just before that when I decide to create that new Tinder profile. It's about to be fall and I want those hoodies; in mid-August my icy cold, and constantly evolving bio is again posted on Tinder with a new smattering of cute summer photos.

My inbox is full of local matches when I leave for the east coast in the last week in September to visit a client along the Jersey Shore and another near Philly. I fly into Newark and rent a car, turning on Tinder in the airport while I move through the steps to get to the rental car aisles, and I leave it on while I drive the hour to my hotel. The first work meetings are that afternoon, so I settle into my room, take a couple of super cute and sexy selfies, update my Tinder profile with the new photos, and drive to my client site. By the time I finish with work for the evening, my inbox is full of new matches up and down the eastern seaboard, alongside a slew of far-flung matches who swiped right while we were passing in the airport, or elsewhere in my travels.

This trip results in several matches that last well into the future and two memorable real-life links with Super Man and the Power Button man. Mr. NYC, Mr. Philly, Mr. Connecticut, and Mr. Iowa, become frequent texting friends on various social media platforms but never real-life connections.

I spend the week in a hotel along the Jersey Shore, my days filled with meetings and my first evening filled with chatter on Tinder and more sexy selfies, including more than a few NSFW pics I can send to my matches to set the stage for meeting. By this time, I have purchased a personal phone and cell service to facilitate sexting with dates and using the mobile version of tinder.

It's a challenge to decide, and I settle in on Super Man first since he's responsive but not overeager. I decide to visit his nearby home on Tuesday evening and send the details to Sir V as a safety precaution.

His room is messy and unkempt, with a tattered superman costume draped over an end table. He wants to smoke bong rips since he's just home from work and, thankfully, fresh out of the shower, so at least he's clean. He loads up fresh hits and we talk about the way weed is smoked now compared to my long-ago youth.

He's young and up-to-date on the current trends like pre-rolled cones that merely need to be filled with ground cannabis flower. I chuckle about my own method of joint rolling, which is older and more refined than his 26 years. I fall into his warm, soft bed and nestle myself in to get comfortable. There are crumbs or debris of some sort on the sheets. It sticks to my bare back.

He is a fitness buff, with an Instagram portraying a mix of sex-positive memes, fitness content, and cosplay. He is muscular and strong, with broad shoulders and a cut waist with 6-pack abs.

We struggle with the condom I brought with me. It's a Magnum, from Amazon, and he's not the first person to suggest it might be counterfeit, since it is overly restrictive. He digs around in a drawer and pulls out his own Magnum, which rolls on easily despite his hefty girth and impressive length.

Like many others, he doesn't last long, and we rest before a second try, which lasts longer but isn't particularly skillful even though it's rather enjoyable, if only because of his substantial girth. There isn't time or energy for more, so we smoke again, and I return to my hotel with an inbox full of messages.

I lock in to see the Power Button on Wednesday evening after work. We exchange Instagram accounts and chat into the night, while I continue a few conversations over on Tinder with those other links for whom I won't have time to meet in real life, but still want to maintain connections for future east coast travels. I exchange social media accounts with the ones I think I want to meet in the future even after I inevitably delete my Tinder account.

By Wednesday evening when the Power Button comes by, I'm hungry for him. Our ongoing chitchat is hot and drives up the anticipation for his arrival. He texts me from the parking lot and I direct him to my room.

When I open the door, I'm speechless. He is extraordinary. Perfectly braided hair, high cheekbones, and dimples that almost erupt from his cheeks with his broad smile. Without a word, he takes me firmly and kisses me all the way to the bed. He kisses deeply and passionately, moving from my lips across my whole body to the wet warmth of the space between my thighs.

He's naturally skilled, and gently caresses me into a comfortable side laying position to exchange simultaneous oral pleasure. An act I normally dislike becomes luxurious and enjoyable with him. His power button tattoo, tucked into the space between his lower abdominals and protruding pelvic bone, flashing at me as he gently rises his hips in rhythmic thrusts. He's in total control of my entire body when he's suddenly kissing me again, and on top of me, making love to me with a passionate depth I've never experienced before, and can't wait to feel again. No other lover has brought this level of passion to my bed.

We lay in the hotel bed afterwards, talking. He wants to know about my marriage and divorce, especially why it ended the way it did. He listens to me unpack the trauma of that nightmare. He's empathetic and compassionate, wiping the tears that inevitably burn my cheeks when the story is told. Softly kissing them one at a time, before falling into another heated round of the most intense and passionate lovemaking. We fall apart from each other on to our backs, our conversation lighter now, but still intensely engaging.

We talk about the other older women he's met–the ones who take him on vacation or purchase expensive gifts. The ones who bring him the most pleasure in the bedroom, and how none compare to what we just did with each other. We almost drift off to sleep together when that last topic of conversation brings him fresh vigor. He tells me he usually doesn't enjoy *soixante-neuf* either and we end up doing it again anyway because we both seem to enjoy it with each other. Before long, we are kissing with a deeply heightened passion that drives our simultaneous and final orgasms to astronomical heights.

I have the most pleasurable experience with him and that power button resonates in my mind's eye as a symbol of the quality of our connection. It evolved into the most passionate and intimate lovemaking, on par with The Best. Exceeding him only in the quality and depth of the personal connection that develops in the spaces between.

When I return home, I get a matching power button tattoo, tucked into the space between my clavicle and shoulder so that it links up to his if we should ever have the privilege of seeing each other again. We remain connected on Instagram, exchanging casual banter, and talking about another encounter, even though it sometimes appears that he has a girlfriend. I see a few random posts of dinner menus and drinks for two and ask but he doesn't really answer the question, instead reserving his replies for appreciation of the stories and photos I post of my own occasional adventures.

Whenever I have a bad link now, I press the button and it brings me back to us, to that pleasure we sparked, to our connection and I learn later that he does the same thing. Sometimes, we just push the button or rub over the spot randomly and think of each other with hopes that it's felt across the distance that separates us.

The following morning, I head out for a second client site and check out of the hotel since I'll be flying out of Philly later in the evening. I get a message from Mr. Connecticut–he really wants to meet me but missed my messages on Tinder mid-week. We exchange phone numbers to improve communication and proceed to cultivate a long-distance relationship where we discover a shared and unique kink that bonds us. Over the course of the next year, we connect on social media. First Snapchat, then Facebook, and eventually by the fall of 2022 we find each other on Instagram, and he approves my follow-request. We still haven't met in real life, but we talk on the phone and video chat occasionally, and at his request, I send him photos and video of my links with other men. He loves it, and he loves me for loving Black men. Our conversation ebbs and flows, sometimes with growing discourse when one of us feels ignored, but always coming back to a love for one another that transcends our distance even though we have yet to meet in real life. He became a steady loving connection throughout the evolution of my story and provides encouragement and support during difficult times hereafter, but ends up blocked in late 2022 after being rude to me about relationship expectations.

Mr. Philly and Mr. NYC are in the same boat as Mr. Connecticut–unable to respond at times that favor them in their bid to meet me. Mr. Philly is a sweet man, and we talk periodically after exchanging phone numbers and connecting on Instagram. He says he's never received intimate photos of his former lovers, and he's never sent one. I think I believe him, so I send him something cute and revealing from the hotel photo shoot. He's floored, enamored, and tempted to book a flight but he never does. We maintain a novel connection chatting about failed dates, and he answers for me when I find myself in a distressing situation the following year, providing moral support and gentle understanding when my own decisions are the problem. I send him more photos over the course of our connection, just pleasant little surprises for which he seems truly grateful and appreciative. He doesn't return the favor but always responds with gratitude, even if he never pulls the trigger on a flight. He's convinced that one day, we will cross paths in a hotel somewhere on the east coast.

The connection with Mr. NYC is hot. Our conversation shifts from Tinder to Instagram, with video chats, virtual sex, and plans to meet so I can surrender to him completely, if only for a weekend. He's confident he can lay me like no other, dominate me, make love to me, all while honoring boundaries, pushing limits, reading the room, and maintaining a no-strings-attached attitude. Our respective travel plans may overlap in Florida in the near future, but we fail to connect in real life, still maintaining that casual sexy banter on Instagram. He remains connected to me with an interest in meeting if we ever end up in the same geography again, but unwilling or perhaps unable to meet me in a beach hotel for a long weekend, even when I offer to pay.

CHAPTER 7

VALIDATION

Back at home, it ebbs closer towards fall, and while I continue to swipe left on the locals, I keep getting new matches and new chats from far-flung men. Philly, NYC, Detroit, and Minneapolis, where I had a long layover on the way home from my east coast work trip. This is how I meet Mr. Liberia.

He's sweet and in love with me instantly. His profile shows him wearing suits and ties, and traveling the world. In reality, he's a simple man working third shift and going to school to get an associate's degree in computer science. He wants to transition to an IT career as soon as he finishes school in the spring. He has a son in Liberia and a daughter in the city where he lives. He is willing and able to drive the five hours to see me as often as I ask him to, so that we can be in love, and he can care for me forever. It sounds cheesy, and impossible. How do you go from seeing someone's photo to a lifetime of dedication?

I can't imagine feeling that way about someone again but a willingness to entertain the idea, to try, has emerged so I agree to set up a video chat. Which leads to a date, and we select a brisk fall evening to attend an event at the local botanical garden. It's a nighttime tour of lights throughout a vast outdoor property following trails and pathways through the trees and around the ponds and fountains, creating more than a few moments for romance. They all fall flat and, even though our conversation is lovely and he's clearly enamored, he never really seizes the moment.

We stroll through the gardens holding hands, sneaking kisses, and exchanging stories about our lives. He's brilliant, and his life story is worthy of its own book because it is filled with more ambition, adventure, and trials and tribulations than one could ever imagine. He gives me a brief history lesson on Liberia through the tale of his own life.

Beyond our storytelling though, the brief moments of affection feel sterile, almost artificial. After the garden tour, we return to my house to link. It's like lovemaking, gentle and sweet, but again, the emotion feels compulsory. He is almost tentative with me, and afterwards, he tucks me in and makes the 5-hour drive home.

The next time we meet, it's in his city. I decide to make a trip to see my long-time best friend who lives about nine hours away. Mr. Liberia lives halfway between, so I arrange to spend a few nights with him along the way. We maintain ongoing casual banter between our meetings so it's easy enough to plan a visit.

We don't do much while we are together this time, but we do spend an afternoon shopping in a cute neighborhood on the local college campus. We stop at the local sex-positive, body-positive adult store to pick up some goodies and bring them back to the house to enhance our planned link. It turns out to be awkward.

Our last encounter happens on the living room floor in his apartment, despite the bed in his room, and involves the small anal plug we picked up earlier at the sex shop. I'm not a fan of anal sex, but I don't mind a little stimulation, and he often expresses interest in more. The plug seems like a good way to explore that boundary with someone who at the very least, I trust. In his enthusiasm though, he pushes it all the way in without warning, or adequate lubrication! Ouch!

After a hasty and immediate removal we return to relatively vanilla sex to finish up before moving to the bed to go to sleep for the night. In the morning, I leave to visit my friend and it's the last time I see him in real life, despite ongoing banter that persists in the social media sphere.

His instant dedication and desire to be in a relationship with me seems impractical given the distance. Still, even though I continue to see other people, we try to meet one more time, in February 2022 for an opera performance. This time, he decides to fly and asks to spend the night, to which I agree. I purchase two tickets to the Friday night performance.

The weather is horrendous, and his flight never makes it off the ground. I head to the opera alone after several failed attempts at finding someone else to join me. Osiris is out of town, Loki is not vaccinated against Covid so he isn't allowed in the venue, and one other prospect who's expressed interest in meeting doesn't reply until after the weekend.

I trade the extra ticket for a seat at Sunday's performance, planning to go again since I have two tickets and no date for the night. We decide against trying another date and instead remain friendly and connected on various social media channels. I am genuinely happy for him when he graduates and makes the transition to an IT job in the spring, but we don't revisit our relationship potential. He's still not the one.

Interspersed in the delicate dance with Mr. Liberia, and really all the other suitors, are a number of random encounters with long time lovers, new lovers, and an unfortunate number of one-time links. One such occurrence involves a random Snapchat addition in the late summer of 2021. He's one of the Gold Standard's friends so I think he'll be just as much fun, and he appears to be glossy like the Gold Standard, but he is not a Que (as in an Omega from the divine nine Black Greek organizations). He invites me to go shopping in Chicago for a weekend, to which I agree. When the weekend comes around, he's in a nearby city instead of

Chicago and wants me to meet him at a hotel. He doesn't have a room but wants to get one and will get one once I'm there. When I pull into the parking lot, he comes outside to check me out. We link quickly when he sits down in the drivers seat of my car, doors open to give some privacy, and he pulls me into his lap. I'm wearing a sundress with no panties, as always, so I sit right onto his erect cock. It's big and I'm wet enough for a few strokes before I stop, stand up, straighten out my clothes, and try to send him inside to get a room.

He asks if we can wait until the 3 pm check-in time and suggests heading to a park to kill some time. There's a disc golf course nearby, and my bag is in the backseat, as always, so I suggest we ride over and play a round. En route, we see a couple fighting in their car, it goes up on the curb and the woman in the passenger seat flings open the door and cartwheels out, tumbling and running along the sidewalk. The driver pulls the door shut and drives off, beer in hand. The rest of this story is worth it just to have the opportunity to witness this unknown chaos.

The whole way to the park, Mr. Snapchat is nervous about how far away we are from the hotel. He tells me he's supposed to be working set-up and takedown for a boxing event at a nearby convention center, and he suddenly has a timeline. We get to the park, and he wants to "park," so we fool around just a little more and then get out of the car to play disc golf.

After four holes, he's insistent that he has to get back to the hotel to sort out the room and get to work. We head back and he goes inside. When he comes out, he suggests we drive around back and park. This time, he wants to finish having sex, but I tell him no. We fool around a little more, but I put him off since we are still in a parking lot outside when we could be in a room inside.

He's had a taste and that's more than he deserves. At my insistence, he finally gets out of the car to go inside the hotel to check-in and promises to be right back. I already know he won't be and I'm not wrong. After five minutes I head to Starbucks, use the bathroom, and order coffee for the hour ride home. He texts me while I am waiting for my drink and says that he needs to head to the event to work and will catch up with me later. He doesn't realize I already left. I head home frustrated. He sends me a text message six months later wanting to finish what we started. I block him immediately.

Another one of the Gold Standard's friends shows up in my social media accounts. This one may have been a tinder match at one point in time, but now, he's a Facebook friend and Instagram follower. He's a Que, too, though, and he's glossy–suits, gold chains and diamonds, even his casual attire is high end, brand name and expertly coordinated from hat to shoes. He's young, extremely tall, fit, and handsome on top of all those glossy qualities that give them that exterior aesthetic appeal.

He can't find his erection, though, and there's nothing I can do to help. He watches pornography for 20 minutes while he attempts to thrust his half-hard member into me without success. He's not embarrassed and is quite comfortable with the idea that he just cannot be sexual with someone unless it is in the context of fully contrived pornography. I don't know what he thinks we are doing but we are not contriving a quality a scene.

An older white woman and young Black man having more or less random sex between strangers should really work out better for both of us, but it turns into nothing at all when he just can't get it up. He leaves without performing and we remain connected in the socials. I am surprised he doesn't block me given the outcome of our encounter. Our ongoing interactions always make me smile as there's simmering sexual tension riding on the surface of every comment or reaction on Facebook.

Also memorable among the encounters in the winter of 2021-2022 is Mr. UK–a vagabond, a skateboarder, a traveling healthcare worker, an artist, an enigma. He's fascinatingly casual in every way, and interested only in the occasional, transactional link, with a little friendly banter before and after. He always hits me up, and he's persistent. He knows the drill since we have been linking since the beginning. He needs to get on my calendar, or I can't see him. He's an international traveler and he's always on the go, usually to London where he grew up, sometimes, domestically. Like Philly, where he owns a home, or various warm escapes where he can ride his boards in the winter. Whenever he's in town though, I know it.

My phone lights up until we have a time and day locked in, and he's careful to confirm the day before, and morning of. He knows exactly how busy I am and wants to be top-of-mind, so I don't schedule over his time slot with work, or other links. He always schedules in the morning around 10 am, the first few times at his place since I still lived in the house with the For Sale sign when we met. Later, it's always at my new place. It works best since I'm usually at my desk in the morning and this minimizes the interruption to my work. He stays fewer than 15 minutes. Most of it comprised of casual banter since he doesn't last more than a minute or two most of the time, although, he does occasionally last far longer. Regardless of the timing, it's always enjoyable, even when it's short lived.

We often exchange travel photos, especially in 2022 when I spend a good deal of my own time traveling, and he persists that spring, coming to see me far more frequently than ever before perhaps sensing my upcoming dissolution. I'm not sure why I even like him given his rudimentary performance, but I think I appreciate how he interacts with me when we travel. He's genuinely interested in sharing his journey and seeing my travels. We seem to bond over our travel adventures.

It's not just my links that are memorable in the summer-fall-winter of 2021. My mom's Tinder experiences are very different from mine–she lives in a small rural town about two hours north of my relatively urban community. She's 72 at this point, so there are fewer overall candidates, but somehow, they are much more interesting, and not necessarily in a good way.

Early on, she matches catfish and falls in love with one fake profile after another. All of them impostors, with the hallmarks of a scam artist–they're local, but from far flung countries and are here living in some rural community as a remote project engineer for an international firm. Or, alternatively, they are traveling out of the country, once it was a man traveling with Doctor's Without Borders (yeah right), and they can't wait to return home to meet her. I tell her repeatedly these men are not real.

She can't or won't believe me, so she's heartbroken a few times when these fellas refuse to meet up in real life or ask for money to travel back to the US after losing their wallet in a taxi, or whatever their sob story might be. That's when she knows it's all lies, and she deletes them.

I went through the same thing with fake profiles, that's how I knew most of these early matches were just chatterboxes looking for someone to scam. She's always angry about it and wants to send them messages outlining their moral failings, logical fallacies, and other flaws. I remind her they literally do not care. She shouldn't waste her breath.

Personally, I suspect them of being human trafficking victims who may win their freedom by landing big fish, but whatever their motivations are, they're everywhere in the dating apps, so caution is always needed. My advice, push to meet them right away and the real men will show up, falls on deaf ears. Despite my obvious success with this method, she remains reluctant to meet people until she's talked with them for quite a long time. Clearly, she needs help with Tinder, and I'm the one who's going to have to provide some level of supervision.

Every time I see her, I take her phone and update her settings to target men age 25 to 55, and then I swipe right on 100% of the profiles. I chat her up to keep her distracted so she doesn't realize what I'm doing until it's too late. She always rips her phone out of my hands, laughing, with a little fake anger.

She matches with dozens of younger men this way, most of whom evaporate after a little chitchat. A couple of whom become trophies. I have to listen to her tell me that if I link with someone 30 years younger, I'll go to jail (um, mom, are you ok?). She also makes sure I know these younger fellas think she has the most amazing body they've ever seen (mother, please stop! Write your own book, damn). I can hear how much she appreciates the attention and validation and I empathize, so I listen. She needs someone who won't judge her and if I can manage to avoid judging my weirder links, I can manage to create this space for my mom to talk about her experiences (while also gagging on a spoon).

When she tells her friends that she's using dating apps, they all tell her online dating is dangerous and regale her with tales of dating gone wrong. Sensationalized stories from the morning news programs about scam artists and serial killers. They have her convinced she's going to end up on someone's dinner plate–with nods to both Hannibal Lechter, a character inspired by the real life Ed Gein, and Jeffery Dahmer.

I assure her it's perfectly safe, and if it's not she'll be back with dad sooner than expected, so it's really a win-win situation. She laughs heartily since it's the kind of joke dad would have liked, and because she's long been admonishing me about online dating safety, to which I have an endless supply of cheeky replies.

I'm not afraid of online dating since the likelihood of two serial killers being in the same place at the same time is incredibly low. It's a joke I also tell more than a few of my dates when they ask if I keep the bodies in the basement or the back yard, remarking on the magical qualities of my entirely private property where my new house is surrounded by a huge yard and a buffer of trees despite being right in town. When I assure her that I share my location and address information when I meet new links, she knows I am lying, and admonishes me. What if I go missing or something goes wrong? I remind her that I'll end up on an episode of Forensic Files, which is my favorite show so it's also a huge win, and that you never know whose episode of Forensic Files it might be–mine or theirs.

This is also how she meets 63-year-old Walter in late 2021, and she's glad to finally find someone her own age after all the silly young random matches she gets from my shenanigans with her settings. She tells me he must be a chemistry teacher, or something, based on his profile picture in what looks like a chemistry lab with a younger person who must be a student. My dad was a teacher, so she is keen to meet educators, and strikes up a conversation with this profile.

When she tells me about him, she mentions that he's close enough, only 88 miles, but she finds it odd that his profile says he lives in Albuquerque. I suggest perhaps that he's on vacation. She's been talking to him for weeks at this point though, way longer than a typical vacation visit, so I ask for screenshots. It's Walter White, from *Breaking Bad*. She doesn't know. I have to tell her. And then, I ask her for screenshots of all of his profile pics which I save as part of my notable profile collection. I kindly suggest it would be great if she could send me a screenshot of all future Tinder matches before she falls in love again. She doesn't, but when she moves to Florida the following year, at least the quality of her matches improves, and she finds herself meeting more people in real life than online.

CHAPTER 8

SERIOUSLY

Keeping up on Tinder chats, scheduling dates, random links, supervising my mom's matches–it all gets to be a little much. So, in the fall of 2021, I decide I'm going to really try to take one of these guys seriously. With the intention of finding a relationship with a man where I can settle into some consistency.

I am still in regular communication with Mr. Connecticut. We can't leave each other alone, but the distance between my midwestern home and his on the east coast is too much to bear. Sometimes, I think he only messages me when he wants to masturbate. The content of our chats is always red hot and centered on our kink. We rarely talk about anything real, and I tell him so, leading to more angst between us. We want each other, need each other, can't stop thinking about each other, but somehow, despite our frequent solo travels, are unable to connect in real life.

I keep swiping for that local match who's on par with the Gold Standard, or Mr. Connecticut who I presume to be just as amazing. I'm looking for one who is not totally destitute, more like a professional peer, maybe even Mr. We Grown, who irons his slacks in the evening to prepare for the next day. He's not really interested in anything besides sex, though. But somewhere in between these beautiful, young men, is the perfect mix of qualities. I can envision myself complimenting someone in partnership, a gentle, secure, lasting love affair with a man my own age.

I swipe on a high school administrator and Coach. He's wearing a purple shirt and tie in one photo and passionately coaching basketball in another. He's very handsome, appears to be in reasonably good shape, and he's my age, which is unusual. I typically match with men half my age, and while I appreciate the aesthetics, they never really align with the qualities I seek in a partner.

This time, though, I am optimistic that we are in a similar life stage. He insists we don't meet at his house the first time. He wants to meet in a hotel parking lot and drive me to his house. I decline and instead invite him to meet me at a local disc golf course if he's concerned about personal safety. He tells me he's encountered stalkers and other unusual women, so he likes to meet in public and agrees to meet me on the course on a brisk fall afternoon. I play a few holes before he shows up and he walks with me while I play a few more.

The coffee he brings is from a gas station, and it's something sweet with milk that I can't tolerate, so I try to be gentle when I tell him it's not going to work for me—the coffee, that is.

He is gorgeous and I let him know by telling him I like my coffee the way I like my men—hot and black. We end up back at his house, and the sex is amazing. His voice is deep and growling as he whispers commands in my ear to work me through each orgasm and all of his favorite positions. It's eruptive, almost a pedestal, and I enjoy it more than I expect to. He's not what he appears, though.

A school administrator on accident, he's a daytime drinker, cigarette smoker, pot smoker, and freely admits to being broke with nothing saved for retirement and no resources to travel. I won't be taking him seriously after all, but for now, I continue to link with him.

The sex is amazing, so we continue to meet at his house occasionally, usually in the afternoon since it's a 45-minute drive. One cold winter morning we decide to have an early morning romp. I show up around 6 am and we head straight to his bedroom.

About 20 minutes into intense lovemaking, we hear someone banging on the door. It's his ex-girlfriend who happens to live down the road. At first, we think we might be hearing things but she's mad, and the knocking escalates to aggressive pounding that can't be ignored. He goes to the living room and tells her to leave through the window, and it seems like she has.

When he returns to the bedroom, he lays down next to me with a heavy sigh. I don't ask any questions. We kiss and move to rekindle that firey encounter that had been so rudely interrupted. She's banging on the door again before we get too involved. He goes outside this time and tells her to leave again. I get dressed and gather my belongings–a sweatshirt and my coffee cup.

When she's been gone for about five minutes, I slip out the door to find a note on my windshield which, without reading, I hand to the Coach before getting in the driver's seat to head home.

About a week later, I receive a letter in the mail with no return address, bearing the name on the property deed to my house, which is the married name I no longer use. The letter is a full page, typed and unsigned, outlining all of the Coach's shortcomings. He owes her money, he targets single moms with kids so he can mooch off them, he has an embarrassing sexually transmitted disease which she does not name, and she advises me that I need to be careful.

I scan the letter and send a copy to him with an inquiry about what I'm reading. He tells me her name and sends me screenshots of his recent text messages with her that include a photo of my car in his driveway that she took on a previous visit. His response is "Oh no, Cheryl, don't" to which she asks, with animosity that is palpable, "don't what?"

She's stalking him, and now she's stalking me, and it's been going on the entire time I have been seeing him.

My car is registered to my maiden name, which I have been using again since the divorce, and it's registered in a different county from where I live so she didn't use that information to track me down. The only way she could have found my address, and my maiden name, was to follow me home the morning she interrupted us. I expect she used my address and online county records to locate a name to whom she could address the letter.

I make a report to the police with a request they contact her and let her know she's not to involve herself with my affairs any further. I am not interested in any sort of drama. The Coach and I remain in contact and discover that one of his former, regular casual partners is a good friend of mine, and my former spouse's hall pass/side piece. Small world.

It is six months before I agree to see him again, though. This time, he has me pull my car into his garage. We only link a handful of times after that encounter. The letter, however, is a centerpiece of conversation with future matches and dates and the first thing to happen that makes me feel like I need to write this book.

In the midst of all this nonsense, I still connect with new matches on Tinder from my fall travels, including Mr. FDNY. A globetrotter who travels for extreme race competitions, and sometimes just for rest and relaxation. He's discovered the joy of traveling to place like Bali and Thailand, Central America, and enjoys frequent trips throughout the continental US.

We spend fall 2021 and winter 2022 exchanging travel pictures with each other. We remain connected with interest in seeing each other again after our first meeting, which occurs on a late fall evening after one of his races in a nearby community. I meet him in his hotel and he's already in the jacuzzi. He always upgrades to a suite so he can soak after his races. He's adding bubble bath for me as soon as I walk in the room, and I slip into the tub.

He's a little older than I am and very professional, after all, he is a New York City fire fighter, with a fit body that shows the bulk of aging. He's handsome and chivalrous, and he rubs my feet while we chat and enjoy the soak. It's not long before my toes are in his mouth. This has never happened before, and I was never sure if I would like it, but I do! It's incredibly sensual and I writhe in ecstasy I am not expecting, which brings heightened pleasure to us both.

He wants to move on in the Jacuzzi, but I lead him to the bed. I learned a long time ago that sex in the water doesn't suit me well. It's like I don't produce sufficient lubrication when I'm underwater so I have a strong preference for drying off before going the distance. It takes some persistence to get him out, but he follows me to the bed, devours me whole before ultimately sliding himself into me with passionate kisses and constant caresses. His size is entirely average, his skill far above average, and the sex is one delicious climax after another until he finishes. We return to the tub and the process repeats itself.

Unfortunately, I can't stay too long, and he must leave in the morning, so we part ways at a responsible time before it gets too late for the one-hour drive home. It's not often I travel for sex, but he came halfway across the country already. I could meet him an hour from my house and for once, it was worth it. He's texting me now, as I write his story, to tell me about a recent trip to Jamaica and keep me informed of his upcoming travels, in case our paths happen to cross again. We are both interested in picking up where we left off, with my toes in his mouth.

Still, I continue to swipe left, and occasionally right, looking for that romance, that link who matches up to the Gold Standard and who has all the best qualities I encounter.

Meanwhile, my mother keeps matching and meeting men way below her worth. She meets a pilot who flies into her local airport and is smitten, even though he's "kind of a dud," in her words. I think it's the plane, which is very much like the one her own father flew way back when, that gives him the initial appeal.

They go on several dates, and I have to hear about the sex, which is lackluster. She tells me how she plans to insist her doctor give her an STI at her next visit. "Mother! You do not want an STI, and you don't have to insist on anything!" I remind her that she wants a SCREENING for sexually transmitted infections (i.e., STIs) and there is no need to insist or demand such tests. Her doctor will willingly and happily order them at her next appointment and review the results with her, as needed.

Despite her assessment of this man as a dud, she keeps seeing him, basically because she feels like she has no other options. Tinder in her geography is full of garbage and by this point, she knows it all too well. He tells her it's not necessary for them to have sex every time they see each other, and she takes him up on this offer before they head out to an NFL game at the local stadium. He relieves himself in front of her before they leave. She's mortified. And much like the advice she often gives me about sucking it up and going on with the date since it's already happening, she ignores the discomfort of this display, and they go to the game. Personally, I would have left him with his dick in his hand and gone to the game by myself, but she feels obligated to complete the date and follow through on her offer to take him to the game.

Inexplicably, she sees him again several times after this, even once while on vacation in Florida in the winter of 2022, and again at her new home in Florida winter of 2023 after she moves there.

It's beyond me why this woman doesn't select better matches when she clearly has options, even if they're in cities a little further away, and especially so when she moves to Florida. She finally stops seeing him when a local fella in her hometown shows interest.

Also a dud, in her estimation, he's a kind man with a big heart and absolutely nothing to offer. He's overweight and suffers with related health issues, including neuropathy in his feet and legs, and has no income besides social security with no retirement plan. She spent a good portion of her recent years nursing my father who was ailing with heart disease, diabetes, and ultimately cancer. She doesn't want to be nursing a partner again in her sunset years, and would rather be traveling, golfing, and enjoying the fruits of a hard life's work. Despite her vocalization of this desire, this need, this want for herself, she continues to see this man until the night he shits in her bed.

Shortly after this incident, in the summer of 2022, she makes the decision to move to Florida to live closer to her sister and brother in The Villages retirement community. She can drive golf carts around town like a proper little old lady, and hopefully meet someone nice with whom she can enjoy her retirement years.

She is unaware of the reputation her new community has until she's there and she sees a meme circulating on Facebook that outlines the various color shower puffs and their correspondence to types of swinging.People in The Villages tie the shower puffs onto their cars and golf carts to let other swingers know–much like how the gays used colored bandanas back in the 1970s–what they're into, like watching, swapping partners, or exploring limits. She thinks it's a silly joke until we see a car in her neighborhood sporting one red and one blue puff on their radio antenna. I snap a photo and make her dig out that meme to check what her neighbors are into. They are soft swap swingers who like to watch each other, or so the meme suggests. Mom remains convinced the shower puffs are used to help people identify their cars and golf carts in crowded parking lots.

CHAPTER 9

BANNED FROM TINDER

In December 2021, I match with a couple of new promising prospects. One of them is on Tinder global and he's matched me from Washington DC. He's a professional pianist and the very last match I send to my social media accounts before I am met with a grey screen on Tinder telling me my account is banned for violation of the platform's terms and conditions in the first week of January. We haven't met in real life, but we continue to chat via Instagram. He's a classical pianist, the kind that plays at Radio City Music Hall and other famous venues. His Instagram is amazing pieces of piano work filmed from above.

He's a virtuoso and he tells me he hears sound in color. I literally crave his hands on my body, to feel his fingers dance across my skin, caressing with each deft fingertip, my face, my neck, my breasts, my entirety. He's utterly delicious to imagine. Our banter is infrequent but when we connect to chat, there's depth beyond the desire. He likes to know about my life and how it's unfolding, my travels, my troubles, and not unlike many of the men I chat with, he lovingly listens when I unload my troubles, like a passing therapist, without sending or asking for risqué photos. Instead, he just wants to hear the stories from my most recent dates.

The other prospect, the one who becomes Couch Guy, is the last Tinder match I meet in real life before the ban. We meet on Christmas Day in 2021 with a series of encounters leading into early 2022. Buckle your seatbelts readers, because this is where the story peaks.

It is January 2022, and I am now banned from Tinder. It is rather unceremonious, with no specific explanation of which term or condition is violated, or what exactly I had done to commit this violation. Tinder's support team responds to my inquiry and protestation with a blanket statement that they take user safety seriously and my account is permanently banned, without any specific information. Without access to Tinder, I try other platforms. Bumble, Hinge, and BLK, among others, to varying degrees of success.

This is when I realize how much I was using and enjoying the platform–there were some 700 plus matches at the time and more than a couple very interesting candidates I was sorry to lose without warning. One I very much want to meet, and date, and fall in love with. The last message I send, which he may never have seen, is my phone number, which I rarely give out. I try to find him on other platforms and see him once, swiping right, but we do not match. He is lost to the ether. I am frustrated. But there are a few latent Tinder matches whose stories persist beyond the ban and intertwine with the stories that flow from these alternative platforms through the rest of this story.

CHAPTER 10

HAWAII

It is Christmas 2021 when a Tinder match with some good conversation turns into a long phone call, which turns into the first meeting with Couch Guy. He presents himself as a wealthy, well-connected music promoter, proclaiming to be the mind behind the original Bonnaroo festival. He is best friends with Maynard from Tool and Brent from the band Mastadon. He talks about partying with big names at big festivals, he has more than one personal assistant, and he brags of his life Hawaii before being stranded on the mainland by Covid. There is often magic in the air between us, but when we meet in the evening on Christmas after the family festivities have died down, my first impression is that he smells like my grandma's house–it's not a compliment, her house smelled like cigarettes and Fabuloso.

Couch Guy is clearly much older than his stated age of 40. His profile photos are him when he was in his thirties, but he is obviously much closer to 50. Uncertainty aside, I give him a chance thinking I might be pleasantly surprised by someone who's unlike most of the other men I meet. On this first meeting in a hotel room, we manage to make it rain in the bathroom because we smoke a joint in there and he wants to run the shower and fan for a while to air out the smell and smoke.

We hang out in the room and talk about our lives, our goals, the places where our paths inevitably crossed–Arizona where we both lived in the late 90s, and the various Phish and Dead & Co. shows throughout the Midwest we both attended. He confidently proclaims his accomplishments, experiences, and successes in an almost ostentatious manner that is both intriguing and mildly annoying–it's actually a giant red flag that I fail to recognize.

When I finally get up to leave, he opens the bathroom to grab his pants and long sleeve shirt which hang on the back of the door, so he can walk me to my car. We discover the steam and heat from the shower saturated the air in the bathroom and created rain that leaves a couple of inches of standing water on the bathroom floor. It is citizen science at its finest.

With hysterical urgency we work together and use towels to soak up the water and bail it into the sink or tub, working hard to minimize any potential damage or water seepage into the floor or room below. After twenty minutes of clean up, he finally puts pants over his athletic shorts, walks me down to the lobby, and escorts me to my car in the parking lot.

All his bragging somehow becomes a little endearing, and we end up meeting several times between Christmas and the first week in January, without ever having sex. He says he really wants to get to know me as a person. A red flag for sure but I don't see it as such at the time and we continue to chat on the phone, exchange messages, and develop a connection.

He stands in my kitchen daydreaming aloud about the life we can build together in his house in Hawaii (that is currently on AirBnB with the proceeds being directed to debt retirement on the substantial mortgage from buying the property and building the house). We can sell my house and kick out the renters at his house in Hawaii and be living there before the kids go back to school in the fall. He suggests we can travel the world to exotic places, with our kids since we both have school-aged children, and retire in luxury wearing matching bathrobes, sitting in matching chaise lounges, watching the sunset over the ocean in the South Pacific.

It seems unreal, magical even, and when he leaves, he ghosts me for more than a month. We have a brief conversation where he tells me he has to leave for Detroit to handle the tragic death of a friend in Michigan, and he texts me that he will call me right back before going silent. Between the compounding insult of being ghosted by someone with whom I think I have a real and growing connection and the recent arrival of the letter from the Coach's stalker in mid-December, I can feel my internal turmoil about to erupt and randomly decide a vacation is in order. In late January, I book a trip to Belize with the intention to chil out on the beach and re-center myself. Later, I figure out that Couch Guy ghosts me because he is in jail for a DUI he receives when he's in Michigan, but he tells me some perfect tale that agrees with my tender sensibilities, and I overlook the six weeks of radio silence without any critical thought.

You would think I have the scams figured out by now. Because I never intend or think I will talk to him again, his contact information is deleted, but when he finally texts me on a Saturday in February, I foolishly answer. At first, I don't know it's him–he just sends a link to an article about Jonathon Fishman's birthday, a niche topic not everyone appreciates, but he knows I'll make the connection. After a long morning of consideration, I look at the link more closely and read the article.

Then I look up the area code and instantly know it's him. I have mostly forgotten him and moved on to other matches after a few weeks of radio silence but decide to reply and tell him if he wants to continue our conversation, he can pick me up the next day and accompany me to the opera. I already have my own ticket.

Remember the failed date with Mr. Liberia? The opera performances are always on Friday night and Sunday noon, so Couch Guy's Saturday reconnection is uncannily timed. He has no idea about the opera when he reaches out to me, or the failed date the night before, but I knew from our earlier conversations that he appreciates the performing arts and would likely agree. He needs to buy his own ticket, and I can make sure they seat us together since I know the folks in the box office; a condition to which he agrees.

He picks me up in a base model Nissan that looks almost like it could be a rental car, devoid of any personal belongings that would indicate it's actually his car. He's careful to open the door for me and tend to all the gentlemanly expectations for a date. The opera is a comedy–*She Loves Me*–and it's hysterical.

There's more of that magic in the air with themes from the opera overlapping and paralleling our own storyline. Our laughter throughout the opera is almost distracting to other guests but we manage to avoid disruption; however, our collective energy is noticeable. We have a fantastic time, so we discuss seeing each other again soon.

He originally messaged me in hopes of asking me to accompany him to a concert in early March, so I let him know we can call it a date. Between the opera and our concert date in March, is my scheduled vacation to Belize–it's the first sign that I am going off the rails, but no one notices me struggling, except perhaps Couch Guy who proceeds to take full advantage of the situation.

We agree to take it easy on communication until I return so he doesn't overwhelm me and distract from the joy of my travels. It's endearing, but it really just creates space for him to continue reaping the benefits of the current couch he is sleeping on, which is a neighbor to his ex-girlfriend. They feel sorry for him and gave him a couch when she kicks him out earlier in the year, and he stays there until he eventually transitions from their couch to mine in the ongoing scam of his life–I learn later in this story that this his MO is to move from one couch to the next, scamming one unsuspecting person after another, for as much luxury living he can trick them into paying for, even when he knows they can't afford the expenses he's racking up on the promise of reimbursement. But I don't learn this about him until our story is done and over. While I'm involved with him, I am blind to the obvious truths. Even when I can clearly see them, and sometimes even articulate my speculation, it's like watching a train wreck. I'm powerless to intervene and stop what I expect to be a tragedy.

It is a few weeks before the planned reconnection with Couch Guy. Fueled by frustration at the low quality of dating prospects, the drama from the Coach and our stalker, and by having been ghosted by someone who seems to actually like me and wants to get to know me, when I decide on a whim to blow my tax refund on vacation. Belize has been on my radar for a few years and a quick check of the travel sites reveal inexpensive flights and hotels, so I book a six-day vacation to Caye Caulker off the coast of Belize City without much additional thought.

I stop seeing matches because I need a negative Covid test to board the plane and don't want to take any chances of contracting Covid before I depart. With the exception of my opera plans which are the weekend before departure, I stop all links and interactions. Masks are still required in the venue, so the risk of attending the opera feels acceptable. For the first time in my life, I am doing something just for me, by myself–it is both irresponsible and necessary. My finances are a mess, and I really shouldn't be spending money this way, but I don't care. I just need to check out for a little while and Belize is the perfect place.

The island life is slow and warm, with nothing much to do but watch the waves roll into the beach, sit on a dock and read, stroll the streets, and perhaps jump from the platform at the Lazy Lizard. The week floats by with snorkeling and beachside massage, and on Friday, I am invited to sail the Caribbean Sea with a couple from the Northwest Territory who live on their boat five months a year. The trip gives me a bad case of possibility thinking–why do I live in winter when I could find a warm place where the climate suits my clothes?

When I return from Belize, I meet up with Couch Guy for the concert he wants me to attend. He, or his company, are the apparent promoters for the band so he has access to tickets and suggests we will have a VIP experience. The opener is terrible, but the headliner is fun, and this is the first stop of their US tour. It's a female group from the UK I have never heard of–Wet

Leg–which surprises me somewhat given his proclaimed association with Bonnaroo, and other large productions. I expect a VIP experience and a more well-known band based on how he portrays himself, but we were just regular concert goers with seats towards the back of the venue.

He prepares me for people who know him to be there, and to want to talk to us, but there are not any familiar faces or friendly greetings. We still have a fantastic time, and that magic is still in the air around our interactions. At times, I feel like I could potentially fall in love and be in a relationship with this man, and then there are these glimpses of chaos and disorganization within him that don't seem to fit his narrative. His mother and sister have restraining orders against him, all his best friends are in "time-out" which is what he says when he ceases communicating with people, and his claims of famous connections, fortunes, and cache continue to fall flat with no actual evidence that any of it is true.

I ask him to make it real–any of it–but at every turn there's an excuse, and a request for me to pay for this or that, along with a cash reimbursement. At least at first there are cash reimbursements. I eventually learn that all the cash reimbursements he makes are funded by money he steals from his previous girlfriend, but in the midst of our growing relationship, I can't see what's really happening. When he runs out of cash and can't steal anymore from her, he starts partial reimbursements from the cash he makes delivering for

DoorDash, a job he keeps hidden from me and everyone else. It is his only source of income and when he can't deliver for DoorDash, he has nothing at all.

By March, I am convinced he is a scam artist and a liar but I am inexplicably unable to break free of his grip on my psyche, even when the reimbursements become nothing but promises as his access to other peoples' money dries up. Before I know it, he is basically living in my house, leaving during all hours of the day and night, sometimes in my car, to "work," whatever that is, and cooking meals, cleaning, doing laundry, but always sleeping on my couch and rarely in my bed.

He claims his work is to raise funds for music festivals, including a new one he has planned to highlight musicians from his home state of Michigan. It is slated to be announced in December of 2022 for an inaugural event over the winter of 2023, and his success in fund raising will pay off in dividends over the next several years to make him a millionaire all over again, or so he claims.

We finally have sex the night before my birthday. It's three months after we first met. It is trash. He is drunk on two bottles of wine, and more of that disorganized chaos comes through, including several key details about criminal activity in his past. He finally discloses his last name when he accidentally refers to himself in the third person, using his last name as a nickname, as it's commonly used by his closest friends. He has been casually hiding his identity from me and since I don't usually ask too many questions, it hasn't been hard. Just a few days ago, he gave me a fake last name. I knew it because there were no search results on google when I used the first name he gave me. The morning after our first encounter, I search the name he used for himself when he was drunk storytelling the night before.

He is the original craigslist rental scammer and served two years in prison for scamming vacation renters by accepting multiple deposits for the same property, which is a rental unit he didn't own himself. He claims he served his time in a halfway house on supervision since his celebrity and financial status kept him out of general population, which I later learn is untrue. He convinces me he never really did anything illegal, and that the news and the court system have it all wrong. He admits to being a plea-baby and opts to plea and serve so he can put the experience behind him and move on.

Like everything else, this story is patently false, unreal, unbelievable, and to me, possibly true based on the foundation of lies he feeds me, so our connection continues to grow even though I admit he is probably a scam artist, and all my friends think so, too.

All these details I learn later on are still unknown to me now, so you, dear reader, know more in this telling of the story than I knew during the living of this story. Hindsight is twenty-twenty, so I can see all my own mistakes now, but at the time, I was fully engulfed in flames. It was a dissolution of my whole life over the course of my post-divorce adjustment.

Couch Guy knows I am falling apart and leverages my weaknesses to his advantage. I pay for for everything–concert tickets, hotel rooms, rental cars, weed, food, gas–living a luxury existence whenever possible. All with the promise of future reimbursement, that I now know I will never receive.

Somehow, while this is happening, I can't or won't be honest with myself, so debt continues to accumulate between the two of us. I even commit to a rather expensive tattoo, paying a $200 down payment on a three-session piece. I'm not entirely sure how I'll pay for it if, and most likely when, Couch Guy doesn't come through with the promised reimbursement. The first session is scheduled for mid-August and will cost $1,200. I expect to pay for it with the cash Couch Guy owes me even though he hasn't paid me back for anything in weeks at this point and I grow increasingly uncomfortable with the amount of debt between us.

He always talks about how he's falling in love with me, and how he can envision our future together. For some reason, even though I say I don't want a relationship with him, or anyone else, and even though I have regular partners I don't wish to give up, he convinces me to give him a chance for 90-days. My agreement comes with his commitment that if we evolve to be in a committed relationship, I need some latitude.

I'm not interested in a polyamorous relationship, but I need a dick punch card or something that allows me to see the Gold Standard, Bubbles, Osiris, and perhaps a new match at least a few times a year. He is confident I will grow to appreciate and love him, and therefore will not feel the need for the validation that comes with matching and linking with hot, young bodies.

He says he can make me feel seen as soon as he feels like our connection is solid and we can be a power couple on the scene since we resonate on this epic frequency where the magic is real and palpable to everyone in the room. I must want to believe the unbelievable, because even as his behavior deteriorates, and he accumulates an astronomical amount of debt with me, we continue our relationship.

I continue select random links in the face of balancing my desire to make it work with Couch Guy, at least long enough to get my money back, and to keep my options open. By this time, I really don't want the type of relationship he's offering, but there's lingering appeal in his vision for our future if things work out and he pays me back what's owed. Eventually, I am just chasing my returns even if I start out with the intention of nurturing our connection into the sweet spot.

In the beginning, Couch Guy never drinks. He claims to only drink on occasion and to be a former smoker. Later, I learn he was arrested for DUI in January, and the real reason for ghosting me because is jail after his DUI arrest, and thus, he is not drinking because he is on a no-drink order. I mistakenly interpret his sobriety as common ground.

Over the course of April, May, and June he manages to run up a huge debt on my American Express, to the tune of $5,000, on the promise of reimbursement that never comes. After my car is totaled in a deer collision in May, while we are on a trip to Michigan for what I think is a vacation (but is really a trip for him to see his probation officer), I end up paying for a rental car for a month.

He tries to convince me not to buy a new car, and that renting is to my advantage, especially since he will pay me back. It's expensive and he's not reimbursing me like he promised, so in June, I purchase a used Range Rover.

A week later, he disappears with my car for a weekend. I should have reported it stolen but he tugs at my heartstrings with a sob story about his adult daughter. He makes dozens of unauthorized charges on my AmEx, which he takes with my permission to use for gas. Many of the charges are reversed by vendors when I call to tell them I am not present with my card and have not authorized it's use in this way, but most of them carry through.

This starts when his adult daughter comes to visit but can't fly back after leaving her identification on the plane. So, I foolishly allow him to take my car and my AmEx to bring her back to Detroit thinking he'll only be gone overnight. He's gone for days. One of the charges is a $550 dinner at a high-end restaurant. I call him as soon as the charge posts and it's obvious that he's been drinking, a lot, and he's not making any sense whatsoever.

He eventually hangs up on me. I call the restaurant and ask if he's there, and if they can have him take my call. He talks to me briefly and again ends the call by hanging up on me without explaining the charges. I call back to the front desk and tell them I am not authorizing the charge since I am not there, and this isn't acceptable. They tell me they can't reverse the charges and I advise them I will report them for fraud if the charge posts. The manager calls me back to assure me the charges will be reversed.

By morning, it's cleared from my account, but that's not the end of the situation. A hotel in his hometown is suspicious when he checks into a room with my card and not me. They call the police, so I end up having to speak with the police and the front desk as part of this drama. He guilts me into approving the room charge since he has no where to stay and the drive back to my house is at least eight hours. I tell him he is required to return the next day with my car and whatever money he owes me.

We argue on the phone for two days after that night while he claims to be sorting out a dramatic situation related to this adult daughter after he discovers she's addicted to drugs on the trip to bring her home. I have sympathy for him since it's his daughter and the drug epidemic is very serious. I offer him more grace then he deserves and give him a soft landing when he finally comes back to my house with my car based on the story of his daughter and her drug addiction.

I later learn the woman with the addiction not his daughter, and he may be involved in human/sex trafficking, and like everything else he's ever said–the explanation is all lies, including the elaborate backstory of her life and the reason he needed to borrow my car in the first place, which was to bring her home. I let the situation go once my car is back in my driveway and my AmEx is back in my wallet with an apology and a promise never to take off with either ever again.

Despite the assurances, he doesn't stop accumulating debt. I write down all the charges from his trip and make it clear, the next thing we do is clear the debt, or we are done. He promises me he can pay me back soon and to give him just a little more time.

He starts drinking more often after this, having cocktails while he cooks dinner for me, and sometimes, I think he may be drinking all day. He ends up drunk enough on one or two occasions that he becomes difficult to deal with–losing track of entire days, argumentative about details and events I clearly remember, but he makes no credible sense with his words. It reminds me of dealing with my elderly grandparents when their alcoholism and dementia merged into the same disease, and I begin to wonder if he's infirm in his mind, suffering from early onset dementia or alcohol dementia. I want to clear the air around his debt before I bring it up.

His debt with me starts with him asking me to pay for a hotel and he gave me cash up front to cover the charge, saying that he wanted me to build my status with the airline linked to my AmEx. After a few occurrences of covering travel or food expenses using my card and receiving cash from him on the spot, he slowly starts to have me pay for things with reimbursement on the backend. He keeps current for a while, never owing me money for more than a day or two.

I never think to question the source of the money, or why he doesn't have consistent access to money or credit so that he can just pay for things himself. He's grooming me without me noticing and eventually he asks me to keep a record of items he needs to reimburse me for. The list becomes impossibly long. Hotel rooms, concert tickets, travel expenses, rental cars, expensive dinners, weed–all on the promise of reimbursement–but often, expenses I would have made anyway, but more frugally without him. He wants to book directly with Marriott to score points, paying the rack rate up to $550 per night in some properties. Normally, I book on Priceline for a third of the cost, or less, and I still stay in four-star properties which is a shared minimum requirement. We are both bougie travelers, but I have always been budget bougie. He is basically riding my coattails and encouraging me to charge exorbitant expenses for "us" on his promise of future reimbursement. I am a fool, being scammed while I watch from the sidelines, knowing it's a scam, telling others he's probably a scam artist, and still following along some false hope for that promised future.

In June, I start to tell him that I am uncomfortable with the ballooning debt between us, and he promises to pay it down and quit adding to the total, but he doesn't. He convinces me banking rules are different in Hawaii and he will have access to his offshore accounts if we can just get there so he can get his Hawaii driver's license reinstated.

It is obvious to me now that he's probably not going to pay me back, but my heart–which is so broken and damaged by the abusive marriage I endured–wants to believe in his fairytale. My logical brain begins to be embarrassed and ashamed of the situation. I'm a smart woman, with a good education, and a good job, and I am being scammed with my own permission. I freely admit it out loud, while it's happening. I tell my mother when I drop off the kids' dog before leaving for Hawaii, I tell my auntie when I visit her, I tell my friends with whom I often share weekend breakfasts, and I even tell my doctor that I think I'm being scammed.

And still, I book first class fare to Honolulu for two in early-July with the intent of staying all month. He promises a check to cover his debt and the airfare will be waiting for me when we land. His personal assistant in Hawaii will see to it. I go to the store before we leave to get him new underwear, tee shirts, and socks, along with some sunscreen, and a few odds and ends I might need for Hawaii. He transitions all his belongings from a beat-up old suitcase to one of my modern, ultralight, roller suitcases for the trip.

He drinks the entire flight, carefully asking a different steward to bring his drink each time so they don't end up limiting him. I don't notice he's doing this until later when I reflect on the entirety of what happened. When we arrive, there is no check, there is no personal assistant, there is no car, there is no hotel, and he has no plan. He convinces me we can spend a night in Waikiki at a Marriot property and visit the DMV and bank the next day. The room costs more than $500 per night and it goes on my AmEx. It's not hard to convince me I need to try and enjoy the evening and watch the sunset on the beach, so we head out onto the beach walk.

He wants to show me some of what Waikiki has to offer before the sun goes down. We wander over to a restaurant he used to work at so he can show me something of his past. The employees there recognize him, and he spends a few minutes talking with them before making a brief introduction. We don't stay long though, and he doesn't ask to be sat even though there are clearly tables available.

Instead, he brings me over to the boardwalk by the restaurant where he is surprised that you can no longer go from the dining area to their stretch of the beach without a room key. He tries to maneuver us around the barriers, but we end up having to leave and walk around the hotel on the public right-of-way between hotels. Despite his claims to have lived in Hawaii immediately before the pandemic, this is the first of many encounters where he appears to be completely unfamiliar with current affairs at various establishments that were once home to him. Not only is the beach access closed from the hotel, but shoreline erosion has cut off the boardwalk entirely and the ocean now laps at the side of the hotel.

He is still a little drunk from the flight, but the effects are wearing off, and on the walk back to the hotel, we encounter a homeless man, dancing on the street to the sounds of a nearby street performer. Couch Guy takes a bottle of vodka from this man's back pocket, twists of the cap, takes a giant swig, screws the cap back on, and returns the bottle, while dancing a little hula and laughing. The homeless man is almost as shocked as I am and more than a little miffed to have a tourist steal his drink–he's chuckling a little as he takes stock of the quantity of vodka left behind.

Couch Guy eventually leads me into the wrong hotel and tries to get up the elevator. It requires a hotel key and ours doesn't work. I tell him the elevators in our hotel do not require a key, and I don't think we are in the correct lobby. He's combative about it and angry at the elevators. I end up dragging him out of the hotel and searching on google maps for the hotel where we are staying. It's two blocks away and I lead him there in his cloudy drunk confusion. He insists on ordering takeout when we get to the lobby and promises to come back downstairs to get it when it's ready.

We order $50 worth of food from an Italian place attached to the hotel and head up to the room where he immediately passes out and sleeps until 4 am. When he wakes up, he eats the cold leftovers from the meal we ordered the night before. I eat mine hot and go to sleep in the bed–he is passed out on the couch, as usual.

The following day, he leaves to deal with his rogue personal assistant and go to the DMV and bank. I work in the hotel room and have my semiannual performance review with my supervisor. My stress spills out and I blowup on her. It's ugly; I have to meet with HR a month later to reconcile, but there are no real consequences. I am really good at my job, and they just want me to be nice and keep showing up for our purpose. Later, I learn that his personal assistant is just another ex-girlfriend to whom he is indebted for more than $80,000.

They have been involved with each other in some toxic codependency for more than 15 years. She may even be a co-conspirator who benefits from his scams since she's reticent when I tell her I filed a police report, and she asks me to leave her name and details out of the conversations with the police. That part comes later. In the middle of this chaos, though, I only know that she's not producing the promised checks and causing Couch Guy more problems than she's solving. He alternates between being angry at her, needing her help, and wanting to show me around Hawaii like we are on vacation. It's a clever ruse to buy time on repaying the debt.

There is still no check when he returns later that day, and no way for him to get an appointment at the DMV in Honolulu, but there are excuses and drama, and more chaos. He has the conviction that if we can get to the island of Kauai, everything will be easier. That's where he lived most of the time he was in Hawaii when he was married–which checks out, he does have an ex-wife and child in Kauai but has been divorced and hasn't seen either of them for 11 years–and he knows the DMV doesn't require appointments on Kauai.

It's the only fruit of the day, so we travel to Kauai after only one day in Waikiki. Of course, the cost is added to his list, and I pay with my AmEx. As it turns out, he has not seen his child since she was a year old and he owes his ex-wife child support, alimony, and more than $100,000. It's not until much later in the story when I learn this information, though, so off I go racking up debt. I pay in the name of allowing Couch Guy the chance to reimburse me and make things right between us so we can retire in paradise together, in matching robes and chaise lounge chairs facing the sunset.

When I connect with his ex-wife later in the story, she tells me that she stopped trying to warn people years ago because once he gets in someone's head, they don't want to hear or see the truth–which is very much my own experience, both during and after.

Once in Kauai, it's the same situation. No car, no hotel, no plan. I get a room for us at a Marriott property for a few nights, at a cost of more than $400 per night and we head out to the most expensive restaurant on the property for a $300 meal. I observe the other guests at the bar where we sit to dine and boldly proclaim that I am probably the only woman sitting at the bar who has a job. Everyone appears to be far more well off than I am, and the gentlemen are clearly more well off than my date, especially considering I'm the one with the AmEx.

We find a couple of AirBnBs after that to minimize the amount he adds to his list over the course of the week while he sorts out his driver's license and gets to the bank. They're tasks which he doesn't pursue with any urgency. I rent a car for the week, too. Another expense to add to the list.

The first AirBnB has a fridge with a few beers and some tequila left behind by previous guests. He drinks most of it and takes what he doesn't when we move on to the next place. We stay on Kauai a few days enjoying the scenery, with him claiming to alternate work with attempts to resolve his driver's license and banking issues, to no avail.

When we are settled into the second AirBnB on a Monday, he promises he'll have it sorted out and takeover paying our way on Wednesday when our current AirBnB and car rental periods end. The day before that, on Tuesday he goes to "work," and I stay at the apartment doing my actual job. When he returns, he tells me he can't cover future expenses as expected and can't reimburse me quite yet.

Instead of staying another few weeks, as planned, he thinks we should return to Honolulu the next day. We can do all the tourist things we missed by coming to Kauai so quickly after arriving, and board the 9:30 pm redeye back to the mainland, on Delta One at a cost of $1,600 per ticket, which he expects I can just put on my AmEx.

I know my card is close to being maxed out at this point. Hawaii is expensive and what started at $5,000 plus the one-way airfare I paid to get us there (an additional $3,000), explode to a total of $15,000 in rooms, cars, weed, and food. And he expects me to spend more to get us back to Honolulu, do the tourist activities like Pearl Harbor, and then book first class tickets home. I know I don't have enough credit to cover the return flights at this point. I have enough miles to cover flights home, though.

I ask him to give me a moment to think it through and I go outside to call my mom. She's not often helpful when I find myself in difficult situations but she lets me air it out and think out-loud so I can hear myself. I decide I need additional moral support and give Sir V a call; he's been privy to this whole story and every nuanced nook and cranny of the deception, so we chat and strategize. I'm angry at myself because I know I am never being repaid, and now, I must deal with an extremely delicate situation with a man who is about to be left at an airport. This is not my first rodeo, so with lessons learned from prior experiences leaving travel companions behind, I sketch out a plan and overthink it just a little before execution.

In an effort to garner up some courage, I make a few other phone calls. Mr. Connecticut has been messaging me all spring and summer, sour that I gave someone a chance when he still wants so badly to be with me, even though he never takes me up on the idea of traveling to meet each other on a warm beach somewhere exotic, perhaps the Bahamas. Back in March, I let him know I was giving Couch Guy 90-days, even though we seem to want different things from a relationship. Mr. Connecticut is crushed and starts tuning into me more seriously, asking me how I am doing and talking with me about my life, outside of sex on a more regular basis. He randomly sent me a Snapchat while I was on the phone with Sir V, so I message him and ask to call him. He says yes and he listens, gently, then encourages me to prioritize myself.

❖❖❖❖❖

I book a flight to Maui on Hawaiian Airlines for the morning and use my miles to book a Delta flight to the mainland for Saturday, with the intention of giving myself a short vacation before heading back home. I go inside and tell Couch Guy that we are done, effective immediately, and we are returning the car in the morning in advance of my 10 am flight from Lihue. He asks where I am going and insists there are no Delta flights at that time that go to Honolulu, or anywhere else really. I don't answer. I just reaffirm that our relationship is over, he is on his own, and I am leaving at 10 am the next day.

We have to leave for the airport at 8 am and I don't care what he does. He obsesses over the airline schedules and figures out I am flying to Maui and badgers me into telling him my plans. It seems safer to just admit that I'm heading there to chill out a few days, than to avoid answering or lying to him based on how he's obsessing in the moment.

After that is settled, he asks if he can take the car for a while, promising to fill it with gas and bring it back by 9 pm. While he's gone, I try to book an AirBnB in Maui and my card declines. The AirBnB operator tells me I need to email them off-platform to confirm the booking. This is a well-known method for scamming vacation renters and AirBnB flashes a warning each time you log in to the platform, that communicating via email is against policy, and increases the likelihood of being scammed since your payments aren't protected. I take it as a sign I should just go home, instead and don't attempt to rebook. Instead, I scan the flight schedule to see if there are options that take me directly from Maui to the mainland.

At the airport the next day, Couch Guy tells me he found someone to book him a flight to Honolulu, but he doesn't have cash to pay to check his suitcase–my suitcase. We are civil to each other, and he keeps grasping at straws to see if he can meet me on the mainland and drive me back to my house, since we flew out of Minneapolis instead of my home airport, and thus, I have quite a drive to collect my kids' dog and return to my house. I decline to inform him when I'll be landing or give him the details necessary for him to meet up with me, though he knows where the car is parked, I doubt he has the resources to actually fly to the mainland–later I learn, I'm not wrong about this.

He's stuck with no money to come back to the mainland, and nowhere to live on the mainland, so he stays in Hawaii. It doesn't take him long to find a new mark and within days, he's scamming a new woman, though I don't learn of this until much later in the story. In the moment, I just know I am done with him.

We head to security after returning the car and the Hawaiian agent by check-in offers to review his itinerary to see if there are better flights. She overheard us talking about how long he was going to have to wait for his flight after I depart, and how much he wants me to opt for a later flight so we can reconnect on the other side of security and continue our conversation. She obviously doesn't know I am trying to get away from him without making a scene. I tell him I have to go to make my flight and get in the line for TSA Pre-check. He goes to see if the agent can get him an earlier flight and it occurs to me, he might try to fly to Maui instead. What if he follows me?

I wait at my gate, nervously watching for him to come through security, and he texts me that his flight is now much earlier, and he wants to talk before I board my plane. He asks me to wait and take a later flight so we can discuss our situation. He is convinced he will pay me back and if I just listen, everything will make sense, and I will understand why he hasn't done so yet, and I will defiantly get reimbursed soon.

When pre-boarding starts, I get on the plane and just shrug at the agent when she looks at me with raised eyebrows–pre-boarding is a travel trick I learn in corporate travel to ensure your carry-on roller bag makes it on the plane before gate agents start requiring plane side check when the overhead bins run out of space. Before we take off, I check the Delta flight schedule and I know if we land on time, there is a chance I can get directly on a Delta flight to L.A. that will connect me to Minneapolis. It looks like there are seats, but I only get one no-fee change and I don't want to risk making the change and missing the flight, so I just leave it alone.

My phone is blowing up with text messages from Couch Guy, but I do not answer any of them. The last message is a plea for me to message him with anything at all, so he knows I am safe. He's boarding his flight in Lihue and needs to turn off his phone but he is sick with worry.

When I land in Maui, I walk directly to the Delta gate with the flight to L.A. I probably look a little messy, and scared, because at this point, I don't actually know where Couch Guy really is. Did he board that flight to Honolulu? Is he following me to Maui? I tell the gate agent I am fleeing a bad Tinder date and I am unsure if he's following me on another flight from Kauai. I ask if she can change my ticket and put me on the flight that is about to leave for the mainland. She looks it up and gives me a seat in the exit aisle, with an admonishment not to move from the gate.

Before she pre-boards the plane five minutes later, she scans my ticket and sends me down the jetway to ensure I am not seen if he does happen to show up in Maui before our departure. I am wheels up before his flight lands in Honolulu. Within three days, he has a condo near the beach and, as it turns out, a new girlfriend in Waikiki who lives in the building next door to his new spot. It's curious how he almost instantly has a place to stay when he was scrambling but couldn't arrange a place for us when we arrived even though he knew we planned to stay for the month.

When I arrive back in Minneapolis, I drive to my mom's house about three hours away. My kids' dog is there, and I need to bring him home with me, but I decide to stay with her a few days to rest and manage the jetlag that comes with the five-hour time difference between Hawaii and the mid-west. Couch Guy and I speak, more like shout, over the phone a few times on the drive and come to a tacit conclusion that we might remain friendly until he's able to reimburse me. He tells me I can turn that "dick faucet" back on and I'm like, "whoa, bro, who's feelings are you trying to hurt here?" Certainly not mine because I don't have any.

Throughout the entirety of our connection, I always remain somewhat standoffish, with a roster in queue. I am still a little unsure if I really want a relationship, and completely unaware that I am being sucked into this wild cycle of debt and deception. When he professes his love for me, I remind him that I don't think I am capable of reciprocating romantic love. I never tell him I love him, even though I do grow to enjoy those magical moments we seem to keep creating together.

Notwithstanding, the infrequency of sexual intimacy between us bothers me. Even though I mention it often, I'm grateful for his actual lack of interest since it appears that he only showers and changes his cloths every four or five days. An observation I make in real time and somehow ignore until afterwards when I question everything and examine every detail in an attempt to figure out how I could have been so foolish. What was I thinking? Even before he owes me a single dollar, he is a walking red flag of warning signs. Warning signs that I acknowledge in real time and discuss with my friends, even my mother. But I am never really honest with anyone about how much money he owes me. It is embarrassing.

Over the course of my connection with Couch Guy, I end up seeing several of my regular links–Osiris, The Gold Standard, Bubbles–since I am not getting enough sex from him. I am constantly reminded of my *use it or lose it* status, so I continue to link without concern for his feelings. He knows about my situation and does nothing to support my needs, so aside from those initial 90 days, I continue to see random links, especially once the debt between us grows to be a point of contention and it's clear that I'll never really be in a relationship. As soon as I am reimbursed, I plan to cut him off, so in late spring, the casual links resume.

During the summer, before we leave for Hawaii, I also link with one new, glorious, international lover who manages to dislocate my jaw with his massive girth and leave me struggling with TMJ for six months. The dick faucet trickles the entire time we are connected, and roars instantly back to life when I return from Hawaii single. Nothing about the frequency of inquiries changes while I'm giving this man his 90-day trial, so resuming business as usual happens naturally as soon as I'm home. I nurture connections but only start honoring requests after it's clear that Couch Guy's dick is trash, and he's not nearly as sexual of a person as I am, despite his claims.

We only have sex three times, all before we go to Hawaii in July, and never while we are in Hawaii. He knew when we met that I had a nonstop stream of suitors, so I don't feel poorly when I let the Gold Standard darken my doorway, or when I see one of my young lovers and his cousin for an afternoon delight after those initial 90-days expire. I even go for massage with Osiris a couple of times over the course of the late spring and summer. He is always curious about my links, and is particularly interested in keeping up with the drama associated with Couch Guy, so he's the first person I see after Hawaii.

I give Couch Guy a chance and it isn't appealing–by the time I start seeing links again in late spring, I only hold on to hope that I will recoup my losses. I am open to the idea that perhaps we will fall in love after our finances are squared up. But with all that money between us, and virtually no sex, I revert to old ways of navigating hookups with a schedule and timeframe, and no feelings because those are gross. I hold on to foolishly placed hope for reimbursement and a potentially future beyond that. By the time I leave him in Hawaii in July, I am completely over the idea of a relationship and just want my money back.

On the way from the airport to my mom's house, I receive several voice messages offering apologies for misunderstanding my financial security and acknowledging the need to pay me back. Couch Guy lives in an alternate reality where he's going to pay me back, his honor as a man stands on this claim.

I come to accept the financial loss, but what I can't accept is the loss of this idea that I deserve to live wherever I want–that possibility thinking–despite the fact that I am co-parenting with a miserable human who wants to make sure I am just as miserable. That was the nature of our marriage, and in divorce, he still maintains a stranglehold on my happiness from which I need to break free. Couch Guy presents himself as the kind of person who can take care of everything, pay for all the costs associated with life and living in Hawaii, for me, for my kids, forever.

My willingness to sink into this fantasy with him is fueled by that possibility thinking I caught in Belize, and my desire is not lessened by the outcome of this relationship. If nothing else, the possibility thinking is stronger than ever without the discord and chaos that seems to follow Couch Guy around. I do want to find someone to spend my life with, but it has to be gentle and quiet, honest and authentic, and characterized by extravagant travels and luxury, even if it's luxury on a budget, just so long as expenses are shared appropriately.

When I finally return all the way home, to my house, I go to visit my kids and bring their dog by to see them at their dad's. On the way there, I decide I need to get fresh ink–a permanent reminder, something that sums up the chaos. As soon as the kids are over the excitement of seeing their dog, they ask about Couch Guy since he had been hanging around the house while they were with me over the summer, and for the first time, they got used to me having what they considered a boyfriend. I let them know he stayed in Hawaii, since he used to live there and wants to live there again anyway, without offering too many details.

And, even though I don't know how or when, I let the kids know it's possible I might end up there eventually all the same. I can't help it. I caught the vibe and need to be there, now, and possibly forever, I just have to figure out how to break free of my home state, and from that iron grip their dad has on my life, and from that chaos that Couch Guy infuses in everything he touches.

I leave the kids' dad's house, take the dog home, and head over to the tattoo shop where I got my matching tattoos with Sir V and the Power Button, and ask to see the gal who does my work. She's busy, as expected, but I just need a tiny piece of flash art. An apprentice gives me a purple outline of the Hawaiian Islands with a butterfly lighting on Kauai where Couch Guy claims to own a house in which we cannot stay, since it's rented out on AirBnB, but will live in when we move to Hawaii together in the fall–another incredible lie that should have been obvious but was somehow real in my fantasy. I need a permanent reminder of the bad decisions I made along this journey so I don't repeat them. Over the next few months, we remain loosely connected and my anger towards him cools off. That magic between us is still there and we settle into a pattern of frequent connections by phone and text. We think we can at least be friends, if not lovers.

CHAPTER 11

BACKBURNER

Iit's late summer in 2022, I am back at home, and there is peace. Just me and my dog for a week before my kids switch from their dad's house to mine for the month of August. I turn the dick faucet up from a trickle to a full stream, reconnecting with links and matches who have been simmering on the backburner while this drama plays out. I am also suffering with more than a little wanderlust.

After Belize, I am constantly on the verge of a perfect vacation. The road trips to Traverse City, Michigan, which were supposed to be romantic and sweet getaways, are really just a cover for Couch Guy to attend hearings related to his DUI earlier that year. They are always fraught with difficulties that require me to pay for everything with that golden promise of reimbursement that never comes.

We also travel to Indiana to see Phish for two of their three nights at Deer Creek. It's super fun, but there is more drama when he tells me his friend will come from Michigan to bring him his misplaced AmEx so he can pay for the room when we check out, along with some dispensary weed from our favorite shop– Lume. We go to the car–a rental I am paying for–in the morning to smoke a joint and walk around the parking lot to look for his friend's car. He takes a call and learns that his friend was pulled over and arrested on his way to the venue, which means, like usual, the cost of everything falls on me, since his AmEx is now in a police property room in Indiana where his friend is sitting in jail for possession due to the weed he was traveling with.

Couch Guy appears to be unconcerned about his friend's very real legal troubles and assures me, he'll make sure nothing bad happens as a result of the arrest. In reality, I think he may have just been holding the phone to his ear and pretending to talk to someone. His friend never left Michigan, and he doesn't really have an AmEx card–it's all part of his elaborate, but completely fabricated, backstory.

Despite his apparent inability to resolve whatever financial challenges that require him to promise reimbursements rather than just paying for various expenses, I believe him when he says his legal team will help his friend. Why won't his legal team help him resolve this issue with his AmEx and access to his bank accounts? These are questions I should, but do not ask in the moment. We check out of the hotel on the way to the show the second night with a plan to drive the five hours home from the venue afterwards. It's not my favorite idea but it's preferable to spending more money on a room which only adds to the substantial and ballooning debt between us that would surely grow with another night in a hotel.

We still take the ill-fated trip to Hawaii despite growing evidence that this is a scam and my now open misgivings about the connection. I return, alone, still not fully requited in my possibility thinking or travel adventures, so, with the enormous number of miles I accrue flying to and from Hawaii and maxing out and then paying off my AmEx (using a home equity line of credit in a way I hadn't intended), I book a trip to Connecticut to see Phish with a fellow Phish Chick I find online. We have the very best time. I use Couch Guy's Marriott number to get good upgrades on my hotel room in Rhode Island the night before the show, and manage to find a cute, young match to visit me. He takes his used condoms with him when he leaves.

In the morning, I catch the eye of a handsome gentleman in the elevator, and he eats me for breakfast. He is navigating a divorce at home in Miami and visiting Rhode Island for business; we exchange numbers and talk by phone a few times afterwards but the opportunity to reconnect doesn't present itself. While we are in his room chitchatting before we link, my phone lights up. Mr. We Grown wants to link, and like so many other times he messages me in 2022, I have to offer him a raincheck. He has uncanny timing and often messages me when I'm out of town or otherwise occupied. After breakfast, the Phish Chick collects me from the hotel, and we head out to Hartford for the show. Couch Guy uses his hotel points to pay for our room there, as a sign of goodwill towards his debt to me, and he checks us in remotely before she and I head to the venue.

In the parking lot before the show, two people who recognize me call out my name to connect with me. One is a disc golfer who is sure she recognizes me from my recent ace photos and congratulates me for the accomplishment, the other an old friend from a long-ago time I barely remember. They confer with each other. The old friend catching my attention and asking loudly, "hey, aren't you Hannah?" The disc golfer notices the exchange and confirms, "yes, that's definitely Hannah!" I'm standing in a bit of a stunned silence as I work out who these women are.

My Phish Chick travel buddy is just laughing at the whole scene since we are in line for the port-a-potty in a parking lot at a Phish show in a state where no one involved in this story lives, aside from Mr. Connecticut, who can't be bothered to see me while I am there. He is a stunning man with a fitness model physique and a huge smile, and at age 36, not too young for a relationship.

We chatter a little more while we wait in line and make a few jokes about the tour plans. Everyone is talking about DICKSwap2.0, the annual orgy afterparty that coincides with the tour closer in Denver over Labor Day weekend. No one can tell if it's real or a joke, but I happen to know it's as real as a heart attack, having recently been added to the Facebook group for the event. So, I tell them as much, and folks in the immediate area are all interested in learning more.

It starts here with some friendly conversation and evolves into shared details and an invitation to join the group. This is how I inadvertently become the co-orgy-nizer of DICKSwap2.0. There are four more shows on my tour before Dick's, which I am only loosely considering at this point, and I am now officially recruiting for the event.

This trip is life-giving and nurturing. It reminds me of the peace I feel when I am first free from the marriage and all the potential that filled my dreams. Where had that gone? I know I began to feel like that potential was fading when I went to Belize in February. The trip was a reminder that I have my own life to live but I return into the chaotic disfunction of the Couch Guy affair.

Mr. Connecticut declines to coordinate his schedule to see me even though I offer to fly into New York the night before the show; without confirmation, I opt to stay in Rhode Island and connect with the Phish Chick instead. How can I expect to find a life partner in this sea of trash? More importantly, why am I even looking for a life partner at all? When I first got divorced, I feels like I am the only person in the world, like I am the one who can make me happiest. What happened? I can't make room in my life for people who don't love me as much as I love myself, yet I keep cramming them into spaces where they clearly don't fit.

When I return from Rhode Island on the last day of July, I prepare for the kids who are due back to my house for the month of August. I focus on arranging the house for their arrival, saving up a few dollars for the first ink session on my sleeve, the one I booked earlier that summer without a clear plan to pay for aside from the reimbursement I never receive. I make plans for the kids to stay with their gramma in mid-August before her planned move to Florida in September. The timeframe overlaps the ink appointment and frees me up for a couple more Phish shows that are within an hour of my house.

Mom's closing date is in late-September so this is the last time the kids will get to experience summer on the lake with gramma. It is a favorite past time the kids share with my parents who often watched them when my ex and I travel to visit family up north. It never fails that he isolates himself in the basement when we arrive at my parents' house. If I spend time with him downstairs, he becomes angry with me and yells for me to leave him alone, instructing me to go upstairs and spend time with my family. Later, after I've done just that, he yells at me for being "too loud" and "too drunk" and that my family, me included, are a bunch of useless alcoholics.

I dread going to my family's home and after a few years, we start coming with the kids and staying an hour or so before I suggest we leave to visit his family and friends on a nearby Indian reservation. We never bring the kids–sometimes we field questions from his relatives about where the kids are and we just tell them my parents wanted to keep them at their house with the extended family. It isn't until after the divorce that I realize he always paints me as a bad person who doesn't want our kids to be with his relatives–he will say anything to make me look bad and avoid accountability for his own actions. I'm grateful for my parents' willingness to watch the kids when this happens, though, and careful to craft ironclad excuses for our need to leave them behind when we travel.

On the surface, everything seems cool and calm, but underneath, I am lonely and sad that I miss out on all the fun that happens at gramma and papa's house: pontooning, fishing, swimming, beach days, sprinklers, campfires, s'mores, sledding, ice skating, ice fishing, and all the holiday fun you can imagine for Christmas, Thanksgiving, Valentine's Day, and the Fourth of July. The kids get the full experience and I try not to show my longing heartbreak for being unable to be there with them–my kids, my nieces and nephews, my parents–time and again we leave after brief pleasantries to assuage my former spouse and minimize the conflict between us.

This last time, it is just gramma and the kids. Papa has been dead for two years and gramma is selling the lake home he built her and setting out for a new life in Florida. I'm thrilled for her, and with the kids and dog safely at gramma's for a final visit, I check out to follow my wanderlust once again.

Even though it's not too far away, I am spending three nights seeing Phish at Alpine Valley Music Theater, so I need mom to watch the kids anyway. It's coincidence that it also aligns with my tattoo schedule, which is fresh on lot at the Phish shows, drawing attention from fellow fans who recognize the Grateful Dead iconography in the new tattoo, even though it's just an outline at this point. Two more sessions are scheduled and there is still no plan to pay for them.

The fresh ink draws welcome attention and I leverage the opportunity to gracefully accept compliments. I also use these connection points to recruit for DICKSwap2.0. After Hartford, the official orgy-nizer reaches out to thank me for referrals he receives from my parking lot recruitment there and he asks me to keep recruiting on the lot for the rest of the tour.

The experiences I have when I see Phish are always amazing and transformative, so despite two planned work trips in September that will keep me on the road for 10 days already, I lock in to see Phish another four times at Dick's Sporting Goods Arena in Denver over Labor Day weekend.

I message my sister's kids who still live there and ask to crash at their place while I'm in town. They are ecstatic to host me. The plan is to fly to Denver for Labor Day and then directly on to Portland for work the following week. Afterwards, I will drive up to my mom's and help her load up the last of her belongings before she heads to Florida. I'll bring them to my house and keep them there until I can deliver them to her in early October, when can I drive down with a load in my car.

I still don't know that I've gone completely off the rails, so I'm planning out my fall activities like my life will go on as usual, with kids and work and life in the city I've called home for the last 11 years.

CHAPTER 12

OFF THE RAILS

It's hard to describe what happens at Phish shows–it is a carnival, circus, parade, and tailgate party in the parking lot before and after. It is a musical performance. It is family. It is home. It is love and it is light. The concerts themselves are almost always magical and over the course of the three-night August run, between the music and the people, and the love and light, I find the uncomfortable truth that I am wildly unhappy, deeply depressed, and unfit for the life I'm living. The petrichor that precedes the rain and the *Petrichor* that bursts forth from the stage as the clouds open up and the air cools brings me to a state where I am certain. I need to be *where the climate suits my clothes*. I need to be warm again.

During the hour in the lot after the Friday evening show, as I wait to exit the crowded parking lot, I connect with a Young Man whose story drives home how grossly underpaid I am in relation to how much and how hard I work. Largely because I constantly push long hours with no backup—a point of contention with my supervisor for more than three years at this point—I realize I need to shift that paradigm. I am exceptionally good at my job, uncharacteristically successful in my field, and I thrive under pressure, especially when I can use my work as an escape from the difficulties in my real life.

I actually verbalize this dynamic to my supervisor several times over the course of these three years while my life implodes—me, my sister, mother-in-law, grandmother-in-law, great uncle, and my dad all got sick in 2018, and all of them except me died over the course of six months in 2019, before this story even starts. I get divorced the following year, during the pandemic, but not because of the pandemic. It is also during this time of my life when, because of my failing personal health, I lose 125 pounds and discover I enjoy the gym, while I also continue to overcommit myself to work.

The dedication allows me to avoid dealing with all the grief and loss, and my supervisor notes my dedication and success, but does not offer a promotion or recognition, which is the point of contention that boils over with her in July of 2022 while I'm in Hawaii. I didn't ask to be promoted, so I don't get one, and clearly am not deserving of one. She promotes my friend and coworker, who I mentor three to five hours a week, instead. No one in the company's leadership offers to lessen my workload or provide support, no one voices concern over the amount of work I take on, and no one really cares if I work myself to death, although I am invited to find another job if I don't care for my current situation. The struggles that start to be obvious when I go to Belize only grow, and by late summer, I am indulging wanderlust and binging on Phish shows, with poor level of impulse control that signifies I need immediate help.

That one weekend, spent at an iconic venue with 30,000 of my very best friends, listening to the message in the music, changes everything, though. I do not link up with anyone, despite being kid-free for the weekend, and a multitude of offers. I focus purely on the music and figuring out the next steps of my life.

My ex comes over between the shows to talk about the start of school in September–his month for the kids– and shares with me his own personal troubles at work, difficulties with the exploding costs of living, and doubts about his ability to afford to live where we are much longer. He thinks about moving somewhere with less expensive housing but isn't sure how to remain engaged with the kids and keep them in their school, and he can't imagine being without them.

He's been fighting against changes to the kids' placement for nearly a year at this point. We know our son struggles in school, and I suspect it is because of the arrangement that requires the kids to move back and forth between houses every Sunday. We manage to agree on a monthly switch in May, and now, I push for what I know he needs. I offer to pay child support directly to him if he takes the kids for fall term—a true school year placement arrangement. I'll sell the house to free up some of my income and make sure he can stay where he's at, close to his job, and close to the kids' schools, and can afford to keep groceries in the house so everyone eats.

He agrees only because he can see I am also struggling, he knows I am angry and grieving over the loss of the family and life I was building with him. Compounded by the unprocessed grief of losing so many extended family members in 2019. He recognizes his role in our family's destruction and knows he has to step up to take the kids. Privately, he admits he wanted to make me unhappy enough to commit suicide so he wouldn't have to be divorced. He just doesn't like me at all and rather than tell me that, he opts to make me as miserable as possible instead.

Eventually, he realizes he enjoys causing me misery, so he never stops being cruel to me no matter how much pain he causes. Publicly, he villainizes me as someone who yells too much, talks too much, talks too loud, wakes up in the morning, wears vests, listens to Phish, and is otherwise a completely unreasonable person. He's obviously the victim and wants everyone to know it, and he'll always take care of his kids no matter what, especially if it makes me look bad.

So, when we come to this tacit agreement in the late summer of 2022, my only request is that he doesn't badmouth me to our kids. I do everything for them and have since the day I became pregnant with our oldest. I make and take them to every appointment, find and enroll them in every enrichment activity, complete all the school paperwork, figure out the bussing system, get them to and from school—everything you can think of related to parenting falls to me. I need a break, not just from work, but from everything and he knows it.

This reinforces the plan to see Phish again over Labor Day weekend in Denver, just two weeks away, and I also lock in a plan to take an extended leave from work. I put my house up for sale and sell or donate all my belongings, squeeze in an ink session with the fella who started my sleeve work in August, place my kids with their dad for the school year with the proposed child support payments, find a place for their dog, take my mom's stuff to Florida, and finally, move to Hawaii for two months. I am officially off the rails.

I need a break where I can give myself adequate rest, adequate nutrition, adequate exercise, and adequate connections—to the earth, to community, to people, and to myself. I need to start therapy again. I have been building a storyboard based on the idea for this novel, I have an idea for an app, I want to learn how to surf, and I want to experience Hawaii on my own terms.

The time between the August Phish shows and the Labor Day weekend shows becomes a mad rush to prepare my house for sale, to prepare for 15 days of travel in September–five for Phish and 10 for business, to close out the work that ultimately results from the business travel, to help my mom with her move to Florida. It is pure chaos. When the end of August comes, the kids are prepared for the changes. Both of them see that I am struggling, and on more than one occasion over that summer, our son asks me if he can stay with his dad. The kids are very understanding.

Their dad accepts several furniture items from my house, and the kids' belongings, for storage in his garage or use in his house. I also give him all the food and pantry staples. He doesn't accept the idea that I might just move, though. He lost his stranglehold and he's desperately trying to keep a grip.

When we agree to the plan, he's despondent and contrite, and says, with tears in his eyes, he will always take his kids no matter what. He apologizes for wasting all those years of my life by treating me so poorly. He also barks at me about being back around in the spring to care for the kids every chance he gets. It's hot and cold, and this is happening no matter what he says. He takes them a day early so I can board a plane for Denver to start my planned travels. As soon as I drop them off, I am unraveling, and there is a lot of line to let out.

My sister's kids are adults now, so when I reach out directly to them and ask to crash at their place, I am not sure what to expect. They're thrilled to have me, and I let them know when I am coming. They promise me a couch and at least a little of their time.

Their mom has been dead for three years now and I arrive the day after what would have been her 46th birthday, so all three of us feel the raw emotion of her loss. It's hidden in the layers of grief that overlap losing my dad the same year, and the dissolution of my marriage and family shortly thereafter. Little do I know that they are layered in their own grief of losing their dad. He's not dead but he turns into a stranger after their mom dies and he abandons them for a new life with an old girlfriend.

The girls, now grown, describe pain and grief that is palpable. Their aunt and uncle–their mom's half siblings–barely speak to them, caught up, far away, in their own families and lives. Their grandfather, their mom's dad and my uncle, is absent. They tell me they feel like they lost their dad along with all their mom's relatives when she died. I am crushed at their heartache and inspired by their strength. They're working, the oldest is enrolled in college, and they live in a nice apartment in the Denver metro. Despite their challenges, I'm optimistic for them but their situation continues to weigh heavily on me. I even consider if relocating to Denver after Hawaii might be my next move. It's too early to tell.

It is unexpectedly therapeutic for the three of us to connect over the weekend and by the time I leave on Monday, I am convinced they don't need me close, as long as we remain connected. The youngest, just 18 years old, drives me to and from the venue on the first night of Phish's four-night Labor Day weekend run and we use that time to chat about her mental health struggles, my own failing mental health, the benefit of having a diagnosis, and how proactively seeking care when you need it can minimize disruptions to your life. The second night, I carpool with friends so I can attend the DICKSwap2.0 afterparty, and I drive myself the last two nights; I'm going solo which doesn't seem like a big deal to me.

Later, a number of my friends mention how impressed they are by my bravery, and I pick up similar vibes from the Phish Chicks on Facebook, many of whom decide not to attend since they don't have a boyfriend or are too sad from recent breakups. That seems silly. I can't understand why going to a show solo is such a big deal, because I don't feel alone. I feel like I am with 40,000 of my best friends. Dick's Sporting Goods Arena is the venue, the parking lot is full, and when the gates open for the sold-out crowd, the air is electric–all four nights I make new friends and connections with the people around me. I am adopted by a fun tour crew based in Denver on the first night and spend portions of the rest of the tour interacting with them and cultivating lasting connections for future show adventures.

The annual orgy afterparty, DICKSwap2.0, scheduled for Friday night, goes off without a hitch, and despite my efforts to recruit more partygoers over the tour, the event is relatively small.

Many people duck out at the last minute when the concert starts late and ends late due to a weather delay, thus delaying the afterparty. Notwithstanding, the event is a success and my efforts to advocate for a sex positive, ethical approach to non-monogamy and recruit on the lot results in being crowned the co-orgy-nizer, and ties me forever into future events with this group. While in attendance, somewhat surprisingly, I do not end up having sex with anyone, instead, I end up nude and fully bound in suspension from the rafters. The truth is, I am not particularly attracted to the typical Phish fan, so this is the perfect way for me to participate in the festivities.

Very few Phish fans fall into my sweet spot, so while I make a ton of new friends each night of the run, I rely on the apps to match and link while I'm in Denver. I connect with Mr. Amway and decide to have coffee and bacon with him on Sunday morning before the show. He lives in a nice house in Denver. This time, I do send the address to Sir V, like I told my mom I do when I visit the homes of strangers I meet online. Breakfast is basic, served on a styrofoam plate, and the coffee is so-so. It's almost as if he doesn't usually cook for anyone even though his kids live with him full time and he claims he cooks. I'm not much for breakfast so it doesn't bother me. I am more interested in the quality of the link.

As always, he is Black and fit, but he's more my age. When I meet men in their forties, or even late-thirties, I am open to the idea that they might be more than a random link, more than a sneaky link, maybe even a potential life partner, but I am never overly optimistic. The hope always leads to disappointment and this time is no exception. The sex is great but before I leave, he makes an entire Amway sales presentation to me and asks me to be part of his network. He's been doing it for about three years and makes close to $500 a month in profit.

He doesn't seem to have other employment prospects and no plan for the future, which allows me to dismiss him as nothing more than a boy-toy. He texts me daily for weeks afterward trying to see me again and failing to understand that I moved on from Denver to Portland on Labor Day, and would literally be moving, even further away, when I depart for Hawaii in October. He is the only link I see in in Denver.

As soon as I land in Portland, I am compulsively swiping for links in the Pacific Northwest. First, I meet a Young Man from the south who coaches basketball for a local private all girls academy. He is persistent in a way that indicates he's probably not very good in bed but he's pleasantly surprising with a focus on pleasing me before he finishes too quickly and leaves. He wants to come again before I leave at the end of the week, but I put him off rather than respond to his frequent requests.

Instead, I want to meet the man from Trinidad–I tend to favor Caribbean men, and like the many others I've already met, he is delicious. He makes evening plans with me that are almost too late for me, and he knows it. Then he shows up even later, cutely quipping that time is an illusion. Based on our initial chat, he seems to be a professional, a homeowner–he tries to get me to come to him but I am exhausted from travel and work, so I ask him to come to me–and he does. He is a beautiful man with perfectly manicured hands and feet, tall and lean, with a mild island accent. He is ethically non-monogamous. Of course he is not single.

He has one other frequent lover, and he quizzes me about my sexuality and recent encounters, my testing status, and about the scrapes he observes on my knee and ankles that come from working on the roof of my house the weekend before I travel. He's concerned they might be from drug use, and he inspects my elbows and toes for needle tracks to make sure I'm not an addict. It's oddly endearing because he does this with compassion and care and ensures me it isn't to be judgmental. He just wants to know the full risk profile.

We lay in bed and talk for an hour before he starts kissing me, caressing me, devouring me, making love to me. It's really lovely and fully engaged pleasure for both of us. The next day, I travel back to the Midwest to move forward with my plans to stage and list the house, take leave from work, help my mom move to Florida, and take myself to Hawaii for a few months. Before I am fully disconnected, Mr. Trinidad messages me that he's concerned about gonorrhea and asks me to get tested. He hasn't been but he's experiencing symptoms and wants us to be safe.

When I see my doctor a few days later, she agrees I need this break and advises me to cancel my second work trip scheduled for the end of September and to stop working as soon as possible. She will approval a medical leave so I can try for short-term disability. She also orders a full panel screening for sexually transmitted infections that comes back negative.

She is worried–I have been treated for infections twice already and I was just tested in August, and aside from that, she can see the stress and grief piling up. With genuine concern asks if I am at risk for suicide. I probably am and can't even lie to myself about it anymore, much less pass off a lie to her–she's been my doctor for 10 years. The weight has become too much to bear. At least I can be honest with myself. I need the break, I need therapy, but I can't just stop work. I have one open report and one deadline that is two weeks out, so I agree to a reduced work schedule for two weeks, and to stop working in early October.

My second ink appointment is set up around my work schedule, so when my plans change, I reach out and ask for a sooner appointment than our plan for October 13, and he invites me to sit on October 1 at a tattoo convention instead–it requires me to sit for 12 hours rather than eight, and I agree since the price is the same, and the timing is better.

I get a hotel room for the night and swipe right on Mr. Haiti. He's a traveling technician so he won't be around for a long time, but he's around for a good time. I can tell by his profile photos that he's a lot of fun with a big personality, so I arrange to meet up with him in my room by the convention center. He's an amazing lover, as island men tend to be, and he devours me whole from the moment he walks in the room. He's tall and broad, with a fitness model body, and a full head of well kept dreads that he wears tied up upon themselves. He doesn't have an island accent, but his voice is deep and mellow. He consumes me with confidence and expertise that leaves me wanting more, and tucks me into bed for the night before he leaves.

The next day, he swings by the booth at the convention to chat before disappearing into the venue to find his own tattoo–a gorilla roaring over his kneecap–which I see in photos on Instagram, but never in real life.

CHAPTER 13

BAD DECISIONS

By late summer 2022, my tag line on Tinder *feelings are gross; don't catch them with me* evolves to *I make bad decisions* on BLK. So, in the spirit of making bad decisions, I answer the phone when Couch Guy calls on a late August evening when he expects me to be sleeping. We are playing phone tag and I am trying to connect with him to let him know my plans.

He's shocked and excited when he hears I am going to be in Hawaii by October 15 and offers me what he calls a "soft landing." He'll pay for my airfare and find me an apartment where I can stay through December, and he will introduce me to an entire network of people with whom I can be friends, so I won't have to worry about building a social life from scratch. I know it's all lies and accept the offer anyway. I make bad decisions.

In September, during the peak of the chaos with my travel, my mom moving, and my own home staging and sale, he calls and asks me to speak to a potential landlord and apply for a rental. They decline my application for someone willing to sign a year-long lease. He assures me not to worry. He has another place lined up for me already, with a friend of his neighbor.

A week later, he asks me for $350. The story is elaborate and fully detailed. He has to pay $6,075 in rent to the landlord of the apartment but he's short, and he has the cash, but he can't load it directly to his CashApp. He reaches the limit when he deposits the first $5,000 on top of the few hundred dollars he already has in his account. He just needs that last $350 to round out the rental payment for my stay. I listen to him tell me the details and then decline to send him the money. I stroke the Hawaii tattoo, prominently placed on my right forearm, and lie to him when I say I don't have that much cash in the bank. The next day, he tells me his neighbor took care of it and he has the apartment paid through December. He can't wait to see me.

I know it's a lie but still want to believe him. There's a part of me that wants to think that he's better, that being in Hawaii is good for him. He seems to have landed on his feet and he is thriving in Waikiki with a condo, time to surf, and is building a foundation to see his daughter more often, or so he claims. He has a vested interest in a comedy club where the owner is a good friend of his who he met through his current girlfriend. His girlfriend is also the neighbor who helped with the $350 thing. They are both among the many people he wants to introduce me to in his network. He is also involved with a sunset cruise where he is part owner and he wants to open another location of the pizza business he launched in Detroit 10 years ago called Hippie's–it's successfully run by his childhood best friend and he claims to be an angel investor with franchise rights. He wants me to believe he's poised for success and that my ongoing friendship can be a partnership in which I recoup what he owes me.

He wants me to work promotions and host the VIP lounge in the comedy club, work the bar on the cruise, and help run the pizzeria operations from a back-of-house standpoint since I have experience working in those spaces. I know better, but still plan to go to Hawaii, with a back-up plan in the event things don't work out as planned. I want him to be ok now that he's back in Hawaii where he reportedly lived pre-pandemic, but I know in my heart he's just a con man telling me more lies, so I am prepared to walk away from him with the first sign of trouble. But still, I go to Hawaii counting on the apartment he shows me via video message.

Before I leave for Hawaii, I have to finalize the arrangements to sell the house, spend a few evenings with my kids, take the dog to the vet so the person who's watching him won't have to pay for those expenses, pack up my mother's belongings and take them to Florida. I plan to fly from Orlando to Honolulu and I make time for one last visit with my roster of regular links.

The first time I saw the Gold Standard in 2020, I savor the link like it is the only chance I will ever have, and every time thereafter is relished as if it is the last time. When he marries his baby mama in 2022, I believe I have already seen him for the last time. He asks to darken my doorway once more when he learns I am leaving town, and I savor him again with more intention than ever, because this might actually be the last time. We talk frequently while I am in Hawaii, and he makes me promise to see him whenever I come to town again. We miss each other, we love each other, and we say so with feeling—he is my first real love after the divorce, the first feelings I allow without censure.

He's not the only one I see, though. Even though it is not being broadcast across the socials, many of my frequent links end up reaching out during this hectic phase, and I make time for one more visit with Mr. UK, Bubbles, Osiris, the Coach, even Mr. We Grown, with his uncanny timing, messages me just a week before I leave, and I see him, but I am unable to fit the Librarian into my schedule before I depart for Florida on October 10. I leave town with an offer on my house and a closing date in early November, and a few rentals booked for my car, which is listed on Turo in Florida since I won't be driving it while I am gone. Things are falling perfectly into place, almost too perfect.

My route takes me through Louisville, where I spend the night with my college roommate and long-time concert bestie. She met Couch Guy when we went to the Indiana Phish shows and she likes him, despite hearing about the mess in Hawaii when I broke things off with him. She's hopeful we might work it out since she wants to see me happy and in love again, after watching all the love drain out of my life with the end of the marriage. I am dead inside, ice cold to the touch, with no expectation of warming up to love when I file for divorce, an all too familiar feeling to someone who is also divorced. Unlike me, she's found who she thinks is her person for this part of her life. They have a sweet baby together and are growing into a loving family. She wants me to find my way back to love.

I remain open to all possible outcomes, but the compulsive swiping only leads to more content—more connections, more stories, more lovers, and now they are in far flung places along the route from my Midwestern home to my mom's new place in Florida. I don't link up with anyone overnight in Louisville, but match with several over the course of the next few days, with latent matches trickling in for months afterwards—in Louisville, Nashville, Atlanta, and Florida, especially Jacksonville and Orlando.

❖❖❖❖❖

I spend a few days in central Florida visiting my mother and her siblings who already live down there. A nice, retired Navy officer offers to come from Jacksonville to the Orlando area to take me on a date. I tell him I want to ride rollercoasters. He laughs a little but when he figures out that I am not joking, he does his homework and makes arrangements to take me to Busch Gardens in Tampa Bay.

My mom walks me out to his truck, where he's waiting to open the door for me. She shakes his hand and tells him she's coming along, too. Thankfully, she's only joking, and everyone is joyful with laughter. He has the biggest smile I have ever seen, and even though his profile specifies that he's 6-foot, 7-inches, his towering height surprises me. I climb in to the open door of his truck and he closes closes it behind me, hugs my mom, and promises to bring me back in one piece later in the evening.

Busch Gardens has the most rollercoasters in Florida. I ride them all and he rides as many as he can. In a few cases, the older coasters cannot accommodate his massive frame. In a few cases, he's feeling nauseous and dizzy from the breakneck pace we move from ride to ride. There are no lines. It is a sprinkling, weekday afternoon about a week after Hurricane Ian roars on shore just south of the park so attendance is low.

When I have ridden all the rides and the park closes for the evening, we stroll back to his truck holding hands and talking about our favorite rides. He knows I plan to leave for Hawaii in a few days and asks if I think we will ever see each other again. I remind him that he picked me up from my mom's house. I'll be there again, and I'll be sure to let him know. He stops at a hotel on the way back to my mom's and takes full advantage of my open willingness to be intimate with him. For the first time ever, I am on the kind of date I want, with the kind of man I want to date, and I may never see him again. I am done making life decisions that center on someone else, though, especially a man. So, despite his desirable qualities, he drops me off at my mom's and I don't talk to him again until December when I return from my Hawaiian hiatus.

A few days later, with Couch Guy on the line, I book and pay for my own flight to Hawaii. He claims he will reimburse me, but I already know he will not. It is October 15 when I arrive in Honolulu. He picks me up from the airport in a black Nissan that appears to be a Turo rental, and the first thing I notice is a pack of cigarettes in the car. He smokes. Of course, he smokes. He told me he is a former smoker, and in retrospect, it's clear that he quit smoking the moment he realizes I do not date smokers and he needs me to want to date him. He probably quit about five minutes before I arrived on our first date.

That's why my first impression of him way back on that late Christmas night is that he smells like my grandma's house. My grandparents were chain smokers and grandma must have washed her floors with Fabuloso, Couch Guy's preferred floor cleaner, I learn when he stays with me and cleans my house. His scent triggers nostalgia when I hug him in the doorway of his hotel room where we meet for the first time because he smells like cigarettes and Fabuloso. He literally smells like my gramma. I overlook this flaw with that openminded outlook that perhaps *my type is my problem*. He is not quite my type, and thus, I give him a chance when I clearly should walk away. And now, here I am in Hawaii, about to find out if he's for real, as if sufficient evidence of his fraud did not yet exist.

Before he takes me up to the apartment where I'll be staying, he takes me to the pool in the building and has me wait while he goes to get the apartment key. When he returns, he finally confirms that he has a girlfriend he is living with and that the apartment I'll be staying in belongs to her friend, who is the landlord he has paid for my accommodations–the soft landing he promised.

I suspect as much about the girlfriend and already asked him a few times before I travel if this is the case, if he is living with a woman or if he has a new girlfriend, but he never confirms or denies his circumstances. I even tell him I am not coming to rekindle our relationship–I emphasize we can be friends if he's genuine in his attempts to reimburse me, but I am not interested in him anymore.

He still doesn't have the key when he comes back to the pool, but he brings me a beach towel. He is waiting for his girlfriend to finish a work call in a few minutes. He leaves me in the pool area again after telling me how relieved he is that I am being cool about his girlfriend, and if our initial meeting goes well, the three of us can go see a comedy show that features a French comedian who is a new friend of his that is tied into his comedy club venture.

I'm lying in the sun to dry off and see planters full of these amazing purple vining plants with little pink flowers. I recognize them as one of the plants I kept alive from my sister's funeral. It's foolish to take this as a sign, but it still makes me feel good, like I am on the right path, even when I have so much doubt in my logical mind. He comes back with his girlfriend and the key, and she and I connect instantly. She's amazing, if not a little tentative and unsure about the connection between me and her Couch Guy.

Couch Guy tells me she knows all about his sketchy past, which is highly detailed in a wild, poorly written blog that is so badly done as to be of questionable validity (in retrospect though, it is probably entirely accurate). I believe his casual dismissal of the contents when I find them on my birthday earlier in the year, and when she finds the blog with my help on a future Thursday morning, she eventually does, too. But for now, she doesn't know about the blog, and as it turns out, she doesn't know anything about everything. He tells me she doesn't know about us as a couple and would probably be angry if she did. He is not wrong, but I play it off even though I know deep down this is the first sign that things are still more lies than truth with him. I'm now playing the role of personal assistant but he's pitching me as a business partner instead, since the role of personal assistant is already filled by his original former girlfriend.

The apartment itself, though is amazing. It's a one-bedroom with a lanai overlooking the canal and Diamond Head National Monument off in the distance, with an amazing view of the sunrise. I spend 30 minutes unpacking my belongings and setting myself up to be comfortable.

I leave a few essential documents and my disc golf bag back in Florida with my mom, but everything else I own is in my luggage. I know this is a crapshoot and it might not work out, but I still act like it will. I liquidate almost everything I own back on the mainland and travel to Hawaii with a large suitcase and large backpack as checked baggage and a small suitcase and small backpack as carry-ons. They contain basically everything I own. A tiny collection of rocks, minerals, and fossils, a few keepsakes, my summer wardrobe, a few items of business attire, and my discs so I can catch a few local rounds all find a place in the apartment.

As I move through the space placing items on shelves or on countertops, I notice that everything is labeled. Every item belongs in a specific place, and that place is labeled with a printed label to the point of being almost absurd. The shelf in the hallway closet where the extra Brita water filters are stored in a bin bears a label that reads "extra Brita filters." Behind each cupboard door, every shelf in every kitchen cabinet, and shelf and every drawer in the bathroom bears the same white label. The same labels my dad used to label everything, a habit he picked up from his stepdad, who labeled everything he owned with his initials using a thick black marker–D.W.

It's another comforting sign I should be dismissing. It's like my sister and my dad are screaming to me from the afterlife and I am misinterpreting their message badly. I see them in these places like it's a good sign, when in reality, perhaps these are signs I shouldn't be there–because there, I am among the dead rather than the living. In retrospect, it's easy to see but in real time, I am blind.

I come to Hawaii to checkout from my own reality so I can focus on myself and my own mental health. I am happy to contribute to Couch Guy's success with his girlfriend and his business ventures if it doesn't interfere with my own purpose, but I know from the beginning something is off. The first few days are amazing.

I take my first therapy appointment sitting on the bed in my room in the middle of the night after scheduling it in the wrong time zone. My therapist is nice but obsessed about my sex life and overemphasizing the risk of pubic contact as reason enough to never engage in sex outside of marriage or a partnership. She's not a good fit for my lifestyle so I don't discuss my sex life with her often, even though it's a crucial part of my wellness. The constant stream of hookups validates me, despite the risks, and that need for validation and visibility, particularly from these younger men. I continue to be surprised by their interest even though I receive constant compliments on my appearance. With confirmation that Couch Guy does indeed have a girlfriend, I turn the dating apps on the next day.

On the first afternoon I am in Waikiki, I walk down to a neighboring hotel where a friend from home is visiting. He has two storefronts selling Delta-8 THC and his sister just opened a location on the Big Island. He's interested in a second Hawaii location, possibly in Honolulu, or potentially on Maui, and wants me to run the store for him. When I get to his room, he is there with a handsome Young Man he picked up at the PRIDE parade the day before and its clear he is in no condition to discuss business in any meaningful way. Lines of coke are laid out on the dresser and the evidence of a raunchy sexual encounter are strewn around the room.

The young guest is a mess and trying to clean up and clear out while my friend and I manage to agree that a storefront in Honolulu is unlikely to be profitable. We table the discussion until we can visit Maui in person. I agree to make an attempt to visit the island while I'm in Hawaii so I can do basic business reconnaissance to assess viability of a Delta-8 storefront there. The visit is short, and I leave so he can reconvene with his date.

For the next few days, I wake up way too early and enjoy the sun rising over Diamond Head, hot coffee on the lanai, and compulsive swiping on dating apps. I take early morning walks along the beach, where I am saddened to see heaps of belongings and passed out people littering the sand in the hours before the tourists emerge from their hotels across the street. Homelessness is a scourge in Honolulu.

There's a bench where I like to sit and watch the ocean in Waikiki–both sunrise and sunset–that I discover during these initial outings when I stop to catch up with dating app chatter. I sit and watch the waves lapping at the beach and I'm troubled by the idea that I can't just walk down to the beach and go swimming. How would I take care of my shoes? I can leave my cellphone and wallet in the apartment, but I still need to take the key and wear glasses and shoes to the beach, so despite the nearly immediate proximity, figuring out where to safely store my belongings while I swim when I am essentially solo perplexes me.

There's a lot of talk about future beach days and surf lessons with the island's most notable pro-surfers that will happen in the days to come, but Couch Guy is busy with "work" most days, as is his girlfriend, who also works from home. It's only been a few days but the inability to get in the ocean is another early sign that things are going awry.

After two relaxation days, I begin writing this book, and Couch Guy starts visiting me for what he calls planning meetings. We discuss the plans for the pizza business in general terms, with work on that project expected to grow as more investments from other partners come through in the coming months. He has very specific plans for the comedy club right now. A big-name comedian is coming to Honolulu to perform at the club where he owns the VIP seats and he's hosting their entourage. This entails booking a room at the Marriott for two nights at a cost of nearly $1,000, chauffeuring them around town, and entertaining them pre- and post-show in the hotel suite. He asks me to book the room with a promise it can be charged to his account at check-in and canceled if needed with 48-hours' notice.

He wants me to spend the days preceding the shows visiting concierges in Waikiki's hotels to generate interest and ticket sales, and to offer free tickets to the workers themselves as a means to ensure ongoing referrals to the comedy club. The next day is Monday so I go set up an account at the local bank he uses so he can set up daily direct deposits of $200 to cover the expenses associated with this proposed work. I make reservations to rent a car the next day, for which he once again promises, I will be reimbursed. I remain largely skeptical since it's not the first time he's promised to make daily deposits, and there is still no clear source of income.

It only takes a few more days for me to see what's happening–he is scamming the lovely woman he now lives with, and his business plans and business deals are tenuous at best. He met this new woman just three days after I left him in Hawaii in July and he is filling her head up with lies. Lies about the apartment he owns in the building next door to hers, which is being renovated, all the money he has in his offshore accounts, how they can live out their lives together on far away beaches in side-by-side chaise lounges and matching bathrobes, living off his millions stashed in the Cayman Islands, with his various personal assistants, who alternately save him and fuck him over, making all the arrangements. It is the exact same life plans he made with me in my Midwest kitchen in January.

She's smitten with him. Her Facebook statuses from time they first met, in July, claim ridiculous happiness. She lets him move in with a promise to pay half her rent until he can get back into his own renovated place. I only see these Facebook updates later in this story, after I meet her and learn her name, and then become suspicious about the level of deception that she's either succumbed to, or in which she is an active participant. She's not friends with him on Facebook, but I find her profile based on her name, and scroll through her statuses out of curiosity. I haven't been connected to him since I left him in Hawaii in July, but when we first met it took months for him to let me into his social media sphere. I take their lack of connection to mean she is being duped. She is in the exact same place I was six months ago wondering what the actual fuck is going on with this man and yet somehow unable to break free from his sea of deception to believe what's plainly clear to everyone else. Couch Guy is a conman.

❖❖❖❖❖

The next day, Couch Guy returns the black Nissan since I am picking up my rental car–for which he will reimburse me, of course. He plans to rent better cars for himself and his girlfriend through Turo once there is money flowing between our bank accounts. Until then, he wants to share the rental I am scheduled to pick up later that afternoon. I already set up the savings and checking account at American Savings Bank and gave him the account information on Monday so he can set up direct deposits along with reimbursements for recent expenditures like my airfare and this rental car. Like I said, it is not the first time he has promised to make deposits to my accounts that never happen, so I'm skeptical.

Still, I reserve an executive rental with National knowing I may end up paying for it in the long run but also expect to appreciate having a car for a few days so I can see more of the island. Couch Guy drives me to the airport and drops me off at the rental counter to go drop off his Turo rental. I drive off the lot in a white 3-series BMW.

It's a Tuesday afternoon in October and we sit on the lanai in my apartment afterwards for far too long discussing business details, my book and app ideas, and his lingering feelings for me, which never really went away. He merely tabled his feelings so he could pursue his new sunset friend. Under other circumstances, our magic could have lasted forever, even though I am emotionally unavailable, and we didn't agree on monogamy. He's planting seeds to reconvene later if his current relationship doesn't work out. I can see this plainly, though, and he still thinks he has me fooled. I am already plotting an exit. There are signs of trouble at every turn.

If you have been following along, you know that 'later' I find out more damning details about this man, and you may have been wondering when those discoveries occur. Now is the point of the story where the truth finally boils over and erupts to cover the entire landscape with his lies. It is all laid bare. Later is now and the details are explosive.

After picking up the BMW and lingering on the lanai for far too long, we show up late for the regular sunset ritual with his girlfriend. She's angry when we arrive and this is when I learn that the landlord, his girlfriend's friend, the woman who owns the apartment I am staying in, is waiting to be paid. I let Couch Guy and his girlfriend work it out on the beach while I watch the sun sink behind the clouds in silence. We walk back to the apartment building together, still silent, and part ways when the elevator stops on the 10th floor where 'my' apartment is located. When I meet with him the next morning, he asks me to send $300 to the landlord to close out the security deposit on the apartment.

In reality, I am paying her for two of the nights I have stayed in her apartment, but that isn't immediately clear at this point. I am suspicious and I can't quite figure out where the deception is happening, but I know something is not right. He says the earlier request for $350 in September, which was taken care of by his neighbor who is actually his girlfriend, was needed to round out the total sum needed to pay through the end of the year. So, why am I now paying for a security deposit? As the truth unfolds, I learn that he has yet to reimburse his girlfriend, even though at the time, he claimed to have cash in-hand. The $350 really only covers the first two nights of my stay and the $50 key deposit. The landlord had not really been paid through the end of the year as he claims. The $300 I give to the landlord that morning covers my stay for Monday and Tuesday evenings–his lies are showing through. I am glad to have already begun strategizing my exodus.

The unfolding of truth happens in slow motion, though, so when he asks me to send the landlord $300, I agree. Partially because I am actually staying in her home at no cost, and because I don't object to paying my own living expenses. And, when I got off the plane, Couch Guy did hand me an ounce of weed, which has a normal value in the $250 range. Like most of the other money he claims he will reimburse, it is money I would have spent, at least in part, anyway. By now, even though I am not yet sure where the deception lies, I know I will never get any of it back, so I do the work to justify the cost and let it go.

Once the landlord is paid, Couch Guy needs to head to "work" so he takes the BMW as he hasn't rented a different car yet–not for himself, and not for his girlfriend. Her car was damaged recently, after which he convinces her to sell it with promises of a rental she can drive until his electric BMW arrives. This is same electric BMW he claims he bought me when I was in the same situation in May with a totaled car.

In a similar fashion, a luxury rental car is the solution, as long as I pay for it now and he can reimburse me later. The difference is that his current girlfriend can't rent a luxury car on the promise of reimbursement, she doesn't have that kind of money, so all she has is the promise of a rental car that never materializes. He tells her when she gets rid of her damaged car in September that they can rent something soon, but he wants her to wait until October and they can share the rented black Nissan until then.

Couch Guy tells his new girlfriend that when his business partner from the mainland arrives–he means me–there will be cash, investment funds for his businesses, an AmEx Black card, and access to executive rentals at National.

Of course, this electric BMW does not really exist. He clearly doesn't have the resources to purchase a luxury car. I don't have the liquid assets or credit he's advertising until and unless my house sells, but she doesn't know that and I have no idea this is the narrative she's been told. So, they share a car while she works from home, and now, we share my rental car that he needs to use to go to "work." It is Wednesday morning, and the chaos is about to peak. My suspicions grow but I am not quite fully aware of the depth and scope of the con. Since my house has not sold yet, I don't have any actual cash or assets to protect, but I am acutely aware that I am being set up to be conned, again.

All along he tells me his "work" is raising capital for events like concerts and festivals. It's work for which he can eventually hire me so I can earn extra income, and it is highly proprietary, requiring a Sensitive Compartmented Information Facility (e.g., a skiff) network. He says he can access these in the business centers of certain Marriott properties to which he can use through his Bonvoy membership. Like so many of his lies, this one has a ring of truth to it. He has platinum status at Bonvoy and qualifies for upgrades whenever we check into a room in their network of properties, including access to private business and concierge lounges. I don't even know they exist until I see them on one of our trips.

Regardless of where we are–my house, AirBnBs, hotels, Hawaii–when he leaves for "work," he says he's going to find a skiff network where he can conduct his business. This where he tells me he is going when he leaves the apartment on that Wednesday morning after I pay the landlord. We have plans for dinner later in the evening with the French comedian we saw the first night I was in town, and who wants to meet at the apartment to talk business with us, the owners of the VIP seats of a local comedy club.

Couch Guy offers to grill supper on the building's pool patio like he often does since moving in with his special sunrise friend. I spend the day drinking coffee, writing on the lanai, and mulling around the current situation. I know it's falling apart, and a graceful exit is probably the best option, if not a likely outcome. When the evening rolls around, Couch Guy calls me to come up to his girlfriend's 15th floor apartment around 4 pm. It's the first and only time I visit her apartment. She makes me another cup of coffee while they drink wine and prepare dinner.

It's a skimpy meal of grilled vegetable skewers and bok choy hearts. I quietly wonder why they aren't preparing something more substantial. Two days earlier, when the three of us grilled out, there were glazes, seafood, vegetables, and beverages—all made from ingredients and items I purchase when Couch Guy takes me to the store so I can grab snack and lunch essentials for my apartment. He asks me to cover the entire grocery bill while we are standing in the checkout line. It's $120 and includes two bottles of wine, on top of the seafood and other meal items. He will reimburse me, of course.

In truth, I don't even mind. They have already fed me two times since I my arrival, so covering the cost of a homemade meal is entirely reasonable. Tonight, I wonder if they hadn't gone to the grocery store for this meal with the French comedian because they have no money and don't want to ask me to pay for groceries again. They should have. The spread is embarrassingly meager, and they both seem somewhat unaware of the deficiency.

While the food is being prepared, the French comedian is texting with Couch Guy's girlfriend to coordinate logistics. He needs a ride and Couch Guy offers to pick him up. He takes the BMW from Waikiki to Diamond Head, and the two of them return an hour later, even though it's only a 15-minute drive each way. Their wine is flowing, and the apartment is lively with casual banter for far too long before the four of us head down to the pool deck to grill. Only after a few sly jokes from the French comedian suggest he's hungry and expecting dinner. Couch Guy and his girlfriend bring almost everything down while the French comedian and I carry a few extras that don't fit in their baskets.

We settle at a table close to one of the grills and they fire up one of them to get things cooking. It is well past 8 pm at this point and the two of them have been drinking since 4 pm. She's not particularly drunk, but he's well on his way to a state I have only seen a few times, and I know things are not going to turn out well.

The French comedian is friendly and talkative, but also indicating some level of discomfort and confusion about the situation that is evolving. He's making jokes, as comedians do, about the incredibly long wait to eat. When they serve each of us a meager plate of grilled vegetables the jokes become more insulting, but they are good humored enough to go unnoticed in the drunken euphoria. I notice in my sobriety that they are scathingly unkind. Many of the jokes are accompanied by sly glances towards me, as if he's assessing my reaction, and perhaps seeking validation that the situation is unusual. We casually push the vegetables off the skewers and our meals are gone in just a few bites.

The conversation turns to the comedy club where Couch Guy "owns" the VIP booths on either side of the stage and with my arrival, I have become a co-owner. He's been telling me we can make $500 per show, two shows a night, by selling the seats through the concierge services at local hotels. The French comedian seems to think otherwise, saying that the club actually struggles to pay their acts and, in his opinion, is poorly (if not passionately) run.

He seems credible, and he is surprised that Couch Guy is unaware of the situation with the club, given his stated ownership share and proclaimed business acumen. Couch Guy's girlfriend backs up the French comedian, reminding him that she's known the owner for a long time, they're friends, and she knows they have never been of significant means. She knows they are currently struggling financially, like many people in the post-pandemic service and entertainment industry. She's even told him that, so she's not sure why he thinks he can make that much money, either.

He back peddles uncomfortably, and this is when I learn the big-name comedian, for whom I have booked into a Marriott suite for the next two nights, has cancelled his performance. I have only hours left to cancel the room without penalty. As it turns out, both Couch Guy and his girlfriend knew yesterday, within a few hours of me booking the room, and neither one bothers to tell me. They both know I have more than

$1,000 pending on my AmEx to cover the room, and that I need to cancel before midnight on Wednesday. It feels insidious that they have not shared this information with me so I can cancel the reservation before it is too late. I make a note to myself that I'll need to bring this up with them later since everyone is drinking now, and I don't want this to devolve into an argument of my own making. It can wait, but I grow suspicious that his girlfriend is more complicit in his deception and schemes than it first appeared.

One of Couch Guy's trademark behaviors when he's drunk is that he starts to make no sense. It actually seems more like dementia than drunkenness to me. A normal conversation suddenly devolves to stutters, random words, and using strange and exaggerated voices. He launches into weird declarations of realities that may have been true at some point in his life but clearly are not current events. Volume escalates with unusual gestures, and he shows timeline confusion. He violently and aggressively dismisses of any sort of rational rebuttal or attempts at discussion when he slips into these drunken blackout stupors.

This starts to slip out as the food is cooking with some silliness about how long it's taking to present grilled vegetables. Has it been five minutes or 35 minutes? Does it matter? It escalates with the conversation about the comedy club where he goes off on a tangent about how he invented VIP packages for LiveNation in the 1990s, a dubious claim at best, that he believes is evidence his plan with the comedy club will work. This causes the French comedian to shoot me more puzzled glances. I return raised eyebrows, miniature shrugs, and odd grins. Even though I have seen him devolve like this before, I am never quite sure what to make of it, but I am sure, he is overselling his own success and the earning potential of the VIP seats in the comedy club.

My own experience with aging relatives, who experienced both alcoholism and dementia, informs my suspicion that he might actually have early onset dementia. He is only 48 yet he acts just like my grandparents did in their eighties, especially when he drinks. I share this concern with my mother before coming to Hawaii but haven't mentioned to him, or anyone else. I do not want him to think this concern is raised out of spite based on our fractured relationship and his huge financial commitment to reimburse me what now totals more than $15,000. It's something I want to talk with him about as a friend once the financial air between us is clear.

The concerning behavior is on full display when the rain drives us all backup to the apartment for the evening, where things only get worse. He is confused and somewhat argumentative, even about going upstairs, despite a consistent windy rain that makes remaining on the pool deck uncomfortable.

The French comedian clearly wants to leave and is trying to navigate this dynamic without making a scene.

It appears he wants to preserve his connection to Couch Guy and feels like excusing himself might become messy. He's probably not wrong so I am glad when he says he has the option to perform a comedy set if we can get him to a nearby comedy club. Everyone agrees to go, and I casually reach directly into Couch Guy's pocket and take the keys to the BMW while he and his girlfriend argue about who's driving.

She wants me to drive since I am completely sober. Couch Guy thinks he is completely sober, too even though he can barely string together sentences. He's shocked when he realizes I have the keys but tones it down when looks at me and sees he can't negotiate with me on this since the car is in my name and he knows I am sober. My eyes, face, posture, energy–it is silent communication that reverberates through the room, and we file out of the apartment with a surprising amount of tempered laughter given the gravity of the situation.

We pile into the car with the French comedian navigating from the front passenger seat. On the way, Couch Guy tries unsuccessfully to roll me a joint in the back seat where he sits with his girlfriend. In the parking lot, his girlfriend and the French comedian get out of the car to go inside while I take the weed and the papers from Couch Guy. He is hopelessly drunk and incapable of the coordination needed to roll. I try to send him inside with the others while I roll and smoke a quick joint, but he doesn't want to get out yet. I assure the comedian and the girlfriend that we will follow behind in just a few minutes.

At this point, he is extremely intoxicated, and he is trying to tell me that if, or more like when, things don't work out with his new girlfriend, he wants us to be together again. It takes forever for him to get the words out and he keeps wanting me to look at him and hold his hand, which makes rolling this joint really hard. I glean his meaning from his posture, and how he's trying to articulate feelings for me in this gentle way that won't trigger my ice-cold deflective exterior, and he's dancing around the topic forever.

Unbeknownst to me, his girlfriend is texting and calling him the whole time to see if we are coming inside or not. She and the French comedian are at the door waiting for us. He's holding his phone in his hand, but he doesn't know it is ringing either. He is barely able to lift his head up and speaking complete sentences is basically out of the question. I let him babble while I think through how I can carefully extract myself from this situation permanently when his girlfriend throws open the back driver's side door.

She opens it as he finally manages to tell me we should be together again. She is livid and I am not sure if she hears his him or not. They have been trying to get a hold of us to see if we were coming in so the French comedian can put us on the guest list. Couch Guy feigns to be taken aback by her anger and tries to say we are having a heart-to-heart, but the words don't make much sense. She can see how intoxicated he is and rather than go inside, she decides they need to go home, instead.

He's instantly combative because we are leaving the French comedian behind. He yells at me not to leave, while she calmly says, let's just go. They bicker and she points out that the French comedian can use a rideshare service. I agree so I put her address into my phone to navigate back to the apartment building. Couch Guy's girlfriend texts the French comedian to let him know I am giving the two of them a ride home and will be back to make sure he has a ride. The French comedian declines the offer and lets us know he plans to use a rideshare service to get home after his comedy set. I am already driving. He's probably grateful. I never see the French comedian again.

On the short drive back to the apartment, Couch Guy and his girlfriend break up in an explosive fight that involves them throwing their keys at each other. She asks him where he will go if he leaves tonight, and he declares that he's going to get in the black Nissan and drive up to his house on the North Shore. The black car was returned two days earlier and he has not had a house on the North Shore for more than a decade. He apparently lived there back in the early 2000s but does not have a place there now. Still, he is convinced he has that black car and a place to go so the two of them are done. We roll around the corner of their block to pull into her garage. The street is filled with police cars. Everything is forgotten.

❖❖❖❖❖

There's a Young Man being arrested on the steps of the corner building where Couch Guy's apartment is located. They both recognize him as the young, gay lover and sometimes roommate of his personal assistant's 19-year-old son. He rents one of the rooms in Couch Guy's apartment while it's being renovated. Apparently, this Young Man has already been arrested twice this week for being a menace and is mentally unstable. Still, they ask me to pull over so they can help him. I maneuver into a parking space just before the entrance to her garage on the right side of the road and Couch Guy gets out of the car to approach the scene.

His girlfriend launches herself into the front with hot panic on her face, "I've never seen him like this before; have you? I don't know what to do." I calmly tell her she needs to get him in bed if she is going to try to reconcile after that mess, but that she's probably better off if she doesn't.

We can see the scene with the police is escalating so she gets out of the car and goes to help him. The police want to arrest him for public intoxication, so she assures them he is fine, and she convinces him to walk away with her. He refuses to get into the car though because now, he's angry at both of us. Her because they broke up and me because I left the French comedian behind. He goes into a corner store that's immediately next door to his building, directly outside the passenger door of my car, and buys a cigar. He's going for a walk.

He walks right back to the police scene on the corner. She has the security fob that opens the gate and is pacing outside the car so I can't park the car quite yet. The police scene continues to play out behind us, on the front steps of 'his' building. I am in the car, waiting for her to decide what to do, and continuing to plan my exit strategy as I watch the scene in the rearview mirror.

The rearview mirror, where this man and this whole situation belong, and where they will be as soon as possible. The irony. But first, I need to find an exit opportunity that involves first collecting my belongings from the tenth floor apartment where I've been staying.

CHAPTER 14

MOMENT OF WEAKNESS

In a moment of weakness, when I can see things devolving further, I get out of the car and approach the scene to speak to the police. I assure them I am completely sober, which is true, and that I can take care of both Couch Guy and this strange Young Man. In what turns out to be another bad decision, they agree to let the two of them leave with me and I attempt to get them in the car so we can ride up to his girlfriend's sixth-floor parking space.

The two men decide they will go for a walk so Couch Guy can smoke his cigar and talk sense into this Young Man, and they will meet us in his girlfriend's 15th floor apartment. Couch Guy and his girlfriend exchange the keys they had heatedly thrown at each other moments earlier so the two men can pass through the various security checkpoints that require a fob for access when they come upstairs. She gets in the front seat of the car, and I finally pull away from the curb with the police watching from the front steps of "his" building on the corner.

The entry to her garage is only 50 feet further down the street on the right, so I pull in only seconds after driving away from the curb with the police still watching, so soon as she activates the security gate. We ride up to the sixth floor and I park the car in her spot, the whole way, we exchange honest truths about our shared concerns–alcoholism, dementia, hygiene, and his apparent lack of money. He hasn't paid her for the rent he promised, which is fine, since she works and paid the rent on her own before they met. I know the feeling. It's not a cost I calculate into his debt, but he stayed in my place for free, too. There are a few other things he owes her for, including that $350 she paid to her landlord friend in September to secure "my" apartment. Couch Guy has also been fronting weed and psychedelic mushrooms from her son and owes him a substantial sum. But still, she has no reason to think he won't repay them.

Words tumble out of my mouth. I tell her he owes me more than $15,000, and that is part of the reason I am back in Hawaii–the lingering false hope he will pay me back as he always promises. He is also promising I'll recoup my losses through our shared business ventures. They seem dubious to me at best, and she agrees that despite all the talk, there has been no progress towards any of his grandiose plans. We dwell for a moment on how he often loses track of time, sometimes whole days seem to evaporate from his experience. We realize he constantly gaslights with declarations that invalidate our perception of events. We wonder how he can remain in the same clothes for several days, sometimes four or five days without showering. I never say anything directly to him about this but occasionally nudge him to the shower when it becomes weird that he hasn't changed clothes. She tells me she has had to directly tell him to shower and change after at least five days in the same clothes.

I mention that wild blog to her and tell her she might want to consider reading it. It's called the *Glistening Quivering Underbelly* and the author seems obsessed with a handful of people and events, one of which is Couch Guy. If you scroll back far enough, there are entries that detail several criminal or questionable events, which, in hindsight sound suspiciously similar to my own experiences with him. She is exhausted and, for the first of many times that evening, she says she just wants to lay down and go to sleep and deal with all of this in the morning.

She is about to broach the topic of my relationship with him–there is a tension building in the air and I can feel the question coming to the surface when the door swings open. The two men come blowing into the living room on the cool night breeze that flows through to the open window. It overlooks the canal that bounds Waikiki opposite the beach, and we can see the mountains beyond the city.

The Young Man from next door is clearly struggling to grasp reality. He's on some sort of psychedelic drug, probably LSD, but it's not entirely clear if that's the only influence on his mental state. I can't get ahold of the situation because Couch Guy is drunk and sucking up the air in the room. He's trying to tell this struggling Young Man what to do in the immediate sense and with his life, overall, but he's wildly intoxicated. He makes no sense, and he can't read the room.

He doesn't realize that the Young Man is beyond his reach, so they're both talking over each other while the girlfriend watches with what looks like horror on her face. She says she just wants to go to bed, again, and I try to get Couch Guy to shut up. The Young Man alternates between trying to climb out the window, punching and choking himself, and talking about transcending realities. The chaos is absolutely epic, and the Young Man decides he needs to go outside again. Couch Guy goes with him.

In the silence they leave behind, she and I manage to exchange a few more details of the deception, and she confirms the name of the blog so she can look it up tomorrow. Couch Guy returns 10 minutes later looking for the car keys. His girlfriend won't give them to him since he's drunk, and he insists he won't drive anywhere, he just needs the keys. He doesn't know the keys are downstairs in the 10th floor apartment where I'm staying. Earlier, she and I agree that is the best place for them when we park the car and come upstairs. They argue again, now over the keys, seeming to have forgotten the breakup that happened only 90 minutes earlier, and things are tense but also fragile. He's leaning and bobbing, barely able to keep his eyes open, his speech slurs and he's drooling. He literally needs go to bed. She suggests that everyone go to bed, but he can't. He needs the keys and he needs to go back by the car where the Young Man is waiting.

I intervene and ask what happened between the two men while he was gone and inquire where he left the Young Man. Couch Guy manages to communicate that he left him at the car when they stopped by to grab a cigarette. He reiterates that he needs the keys so he can get his cigarettes out of the car, and he promises he won't drive. He keeps looking at his girlfriend for answers because he still does not realize I have the keys downstairs. She cautiously observers our interaction, perhaps jealous or maybe envious of my ability to get his attention, force him to focus, and, to some extent, follow through with basic responses despite his drunken stupor. I suggest, and everyone agrees, that I go down and open the car so the Young Man can have a cigarette while the two of them go to bed. We can all reconvene in the morning.

❖❖❖❖❖❖

When I get to the car, after first stopping in my apartment on the 10th floor to grab the keys, the Young Man is already gone. I walk around a little bit looking for him but give up quickly and go back to my apartment. Before I go to bed, I spend 20 minutes repacking my belongings. In the morning, I can shower, finish packing, and slip out unnoticed. I'm an early riser and expect sleep to be elusive. In the morning, I'll find a short-term AirBnB to hold me over until I secure a monthly rental or some other agreeable living arrangement. As soon as I get that straightened out, I can return this car and either walk, use public transportation, or rideshare for the rest of my stay, which I expect to extend into December.

I lay down in the bed intent on sleeping at least a little now that I have a strategy in place. It is well past midnight when I drift off into a light sleep. As expected, I am up early at 4 am, alternately talking to my mom for moral support and my realtor because the sale of my house fell through. They're both on the mainland, five or six hours ahead, so I know they'll be awake when I call them. It really just puts off the inevitable. I have to get out of this situation and the longer I wait, the more likely it becomes that there will be drama associated with my exit.

CHAPTER 15

IT ALL FALLS APART

Before the sun rises, I shower and walk downstairs to let the security officer know I am checking out of an AirBnB and leaving the garage in a rented BMW without a key fob since I am leaving the key in the apartment. I expect to be on the move within the hour. I need them to open the gate for me when I come down the ramp since the key fob will be left in the apartment. I want to minimize the chance I'll run into them on the way out, but I don't mention it to the security guards. I just confirm my request and go back to the apartment.

When I get back upstairs, I finish up packing the last of my belongings when, much earlier than I expect, his girlfriend starts texting me with more questions. She wants to come downstairs to talk as soon as possible. She read that wild blog and has major concerns. Who wouldn't? I know I was nearly terrified when I first saw it myself since it suggests he is HIV+, but he explains it away with smooth talk and lies interspersed with truths he can document with photos from his past. We had sex the night before for the first time and he finished inside. He was mortified to discover that detail but assures me I have nothing to be worried about. He never gets tested, but I continue to test negative on a quarterly basis more than a year after our last encounter.

We are still newly acquainted when I discover the blog in March, so I listen to his explanations with trust and believe him. When I ask questions, like his full name and birthdate, he tells me the truth. He has me on the hook. He knows it. This is when the grooming starts, but in July of the same year, when I tell his new girlfriend about the blog, I know every word of it is probably true.

It's Thursday morning. Less than 48 hours from when this pot started to boil over with the late arrival to their sunset ritual on Tuesday and the subsequent discovery of the unpaid landlord, when it all falls apart. Dozens of new matches are lingering in my dating apps, greetings unanswered, as I ignore all dating platforms while this plays out and I flee the drama.

His girlfriend must have messaged me from the elevator. She's at my door within seconds. I open when she knocks and she comes inside and sits on the floor across the coffee table from where I sit on the couch, unaware that I am completely packed and ready to leave. My suitcases and backpacks are around the corner in the bedroom out of sight. She tells me he's awake and it seems like he's still drunk, but he's lying down in bed, and she thinks he will go back to sleep. The blog scares her, especially the part where there is a suggestion that he has a sexually transmitted infection. I give her a timeline of my encounters with him and let her know my subsequent test results have been normal, and that despite his promises, he never gets himself tested.

She and I exchange a few more stories about our curious interactions with Couch Guy, starting with the details and timeline of when he and I had been together. This is when I discover he met her only three days after I left him in Kauai in July. They start living together almost immediately due to the claims of renovation in his own apartment. All along he promises to pay half her rent–he's three months behind at this point. She is still without a car and still waiting for him to get her a rental car. He told her as soon as I arrived on island, he would be situated to pay her the months of promised rent, reimburse other expenses he owes her, and rent her a car to use until she decides if she wants to buy one.

Neither one of us understands what he actually does for "work," but he tells us both the same thing about the skiff and the "cap raises" he's doing to fund a new music festival in Michigan that will be announced in December and held in the following year in December of 2023. Nor do we understand where he gets the occasional cash he uses to buy groceries or put gas in the car, something he's done for both of us. We have other questions about the stories he tells: his famous friends, his mysterious personal assistant whose son rents a room from him in his under-renovation apartment next door; his adult daughter, the drug addict, who is apparently living in her own apartment in the building next door (an apartment he claims to pay for); his younger daughter who neither of us have ever met–but with whom he apparently spends a week in early October surfing in Waikiki. Or so he tells me when he finally answers after the week of radio silence right before I am scheduled to depart the mainland for my move to Hawaii. I spent an anxious week waiting to hear from him before booking my flight since he promises to book and pay for it as soon as I tell him I am coming. All along I know it will never happen and I am prepared to book and pay for the flight myself.

When he finally answers my call the night before I depart, he offers this heartless explanation of surfing with his daughter all week and walks me through the last minute booking my own flight using points to upgrade to Delta One, promising the whole time to reimburse me the expense. His girlfriend confirms his daughter was not there with them at that time, and that instead, they were together doing their normal thing–living at her apartment, going to work, meeting for sunset, drinking too much wine, and eating indulgently. He came into her life and slowly eroded her routines with indulgence.

❖❖❖❖❖

We know there are numerous lies, and at this point, I know everything he has ever said is a lie, and everything he will say is a lie. She is still convinced this cannot be what it seems–she's the current mark of a lifelong conman who has a long list of women to whom he owes tens of thousands of dollars, each. Among them are his ex-wife, his personal assistant who is later revealed to be just another ex-girlfriend to whom he's massively indebted, the woman he was living with in Wisconsin when I first meet him, and me, his reported business partner. I knew about these and other women from reading the blog, and from his own admissions, but the scale to which he is indebted to us, collectively, is not yet fully understood.

When it's clear that I can't really help her, I let her know I plan to leave the apartment, and in doing so, cut all ties with him, his schemes, and her, if she opts to remain in a relationship with him. I didn't come to Hawaii for this nonsense, and I won't remain connected to them any longer. This doesn't serve my purpose. Without intention of offense, I let her know I am blocking them both and moving on with my life as soon as I pull out of the garage.

We talk about the need for me to make two trips from the apartment to the car with my suitcases and she agrees to go back to her apartment and keep Couch Guy busy so I can load up the car and leave without having to interact with him further. It appears likely that she will maintain her connection to him, probably with false hopes that she and her son will be reimbursed what's owed them. I don't think she is being honest with me, or herself, about how much money she's spent on empty promises of reimbursement. She's chasing her loses. We hug and she goes upstairs.

In a split-second decision, I end up donning my expedition backpack over my crossbody purse, and then wearing my smaller backpack backwards, so I can roll my two suitcases and head down to the car in one trip. My phone vibrates in my purse, I can't get to it to check it, but I already know. She's back in her apartment and he's not there. It's too late. I am already out of the elevator on the sixth floor and before I can react, the BMW senses the keys in my purse and flashes to life, unlocking the doors–a convenience feature of luxury cars I presently detest. He's standing behind the car, facing away from me. He turns around when he hears the car unlock and sees me.

Lies immediately come spilling out of his mouth. He's upset that she and I spent time talking without him. He tells me she needs to get used to the idea that big changes are coming before he even notices that I am loading my suitcases into the backseat. He asks what I am doing so I tell him I am disengaging from this situation and bugging out. I cannot continue to be connected to him and his drama. He tells me I can't leave. He is going upstairs to get his suitcase, my suitcase–the one he acquired on our July trip when I left him in Hawaii in the first place–and he's coming with me. He's done with her, and we need to recommence our own relationship. I tell him "No. That is not what is happening."

He is shellshocked and reeling for purchase. I am sitting in the driver's seat now, my belongings in the back seat, the car is running, and he is standing so that I can't shut the door to drive away. He is talking rapidly, all lies of course.

He tells me if I leave, I will be stuck back in the Midwest, in the pits of hell, with no exit strategy, while he'll be in paradise. He's insistent that my regrets will hit home in February when winter feels the longest. I just stare at him with wide eyes and sly grin, allowing his words to fall into empty space where no one is listening. I wait for the right moment to cut him off with a closed door. It finally comes when the elevator doors open behind him and his girlfriend appears. Or his ex-girlfriend? At this point I am not sure what will become of them, and I don't really care. I just need to leave. This situation does not serve me.

She speaks his name, and he turns around, stepping out of the door's pathway. In an instant, I reach out and pull the door closed while I put the car into gear and roll out of the parking space with him shouting at me in the rear-view mirror. Where he belongs.

It's been far longer than the hour I mentioned to the security officers but, they see me rolling down to the first level and the gate is open when I get there, so I don't even have to slow down to roll out onto the Ala Wai Boulevard.

Unsure of what comes next, I take a long drive to East Honolulu, contemplating next steps. My phone is blowing up because I foolishly did not actually block either one of them. He and I exchange a few messages and it's clearly serving no purpose. He wishes me safe travels when I tell him the sale of my house falls through, assuming that without him, and without the sale, I have no other option but to give up on Hawaii.

I have no intention of returning to the mainland just because I am moving on from this nonsense and back to square one on the sale of my house. I block him. His girlfriend reaches out to me and lets me know she wants to stop communicating with me, which is clearly part of my original plan, so it works out for everyone.

Eventually, I turn around and go back towards Waikiki. Even though things imploded there, this is the area I am most familiar with and the only place where I see AirBnBs I can rent for a few days at a time. I don't know it yet, but recent regulations on AirBnBs restrict their availability throughout the city of Honolulu. I decide on a place that is just off the Ala Wai Boulevard, down the road from where they stay, but in what feels like a familiar zone. It's risky, but it makes the most sense to me, so I find a place to park the car and wait for the rental to be ready.

I request an early check in but it's only 10 am and the best I can hope for is noon, so I want to take a walk around town and just enjoy the weather and my newfound peace. It's not safe to leave valuables where they're visible when the car is parked on the side of the street in Waikiki, so I open the trunk to move my suitcases from the back seat to the trunk.

❖❖❖❖❖

Another piece of the puzzle falls into place. The trunk is full of DoorDash delivery boxes and bags. Now I know where he gets the nominal sums of cash for groceries and gas. He has been DoorDashing, most recently in my rented 3-series BMW, but it is also immediately clear that he used my car for DoorDash when we were together earlier this year on the mainland. DoorDash is the source of the occasional cash he uses to buy groceries or put gas in my car (and her car), and what he is doing when he says he's at "work."

It makes so much sense. He is always bragging about how he set up his adult "daughter" to DoorDash as a to supplement her income, and while that may be true, he clearly also delivers for DoorDash. Perhaps this explains the lack of food when we supped with the French comedian. He didn't have unlimited access to a car to make deliveries since he was relying on my BMW and therefore, had no money to get groceries in the time leading up to the diner. His girlfriend may have had money for such things but was probably unaware of this gap in his funds, and as a lifelong vegetarian, doesn't mind the minimal fare served that evening.

I stand on the side of the road in Waikiki, holding this cardboard box full of insulated DoorDash bags, belly laughing. It's so clear that this has all been lies from the beginning, and even though I knew that already, in that moment the scale of his deception is somehow hysterical.

After I transfer my luggage to the trunk and leave the DoorDash evidence on the curb, I take a walk to the beach and sit on the bench where I like to watch the ocean. I catch up on those smoldering chats in the dating apps. I arrange to pick up a handsome Young Man from Fiji to run him to the grocery store and a haircut appointment in exchange for helping me carry my luggage up to my room in the new AirBnB spot. While we chat, I get an AirBnB notification that the room is ready.

I stop in the AirBnB to use the bathroom and get a feel for the property before I pick Mr. Fiji up from his apartment. He offers to let me move in with him if don't mind sleeping on the floor since he doesn't have a bed. His place is actually completely empty.

We go to the grocery store and pick up lunch. We eat in the car while he waits for a haircut appointment, after which we head over to the AirBnB. After bringing the luggage upstairs, we drive around the neighborhood to find a parking spot for the car about a block away. We walk back to the building and take the elevator up to my room where he crawls into bed with me.

We proceed to link a couple of times, and then lay in bed talking about the world and places he's traveled. We chatter about the simplicity of his life and how his upbringing in Fiji influences how he lives. He's an army veteran and works security at the Louis Vuitton stores in Waikiki. When he's not at work he likes to go to the beach, far from the tourist beaches where the water tastes like sunscreen.

After twenty minutes, he gets up, dresses, and heads back to his empty apartment via bus since it's too far for him to walk. It's after dark and he can see that I am drifting off to sleep. I end up awake for a while after he leaves, so I put on Forensic Files, look at short-term rentals, and catch up on messages in the dating apps. Mr. Fiji messages me occasionally, trying to reconnect, but the timing never works out. Every so often when I walk around Waikiki over the course of the next six weeks, I see him at work, where he wears a suit and looks stoic, but offers me a grin and a wave when he sees me. He's stunning, especially in those suits, and he's kinder than most of the men I meet on the apps.

I wake up at 3 o'clock the morning and the TV is still tuned to the same station. The national news is on now even though the sun is hours from rising. The time zones create a dystopian feel when the east coast news comes on at 2 am. I turn it off and try to go back to sleep but I am still jet lagged.

I toss and turn for a while before grabbing my phone and to find the nearest Starbucks. It opens in 20 minutes. I decide to get up, shower, and go for a walk that takes me past the shop to grab coffee so I can watch the sunrise over Diamond Head. As I walk down Kalakaua Avenue towards the Starbucks in the Royal Hawaiian Center in the early morning twilight, I hear my name come from a cluster of young homeless men.

"Hey, I recognize you! Hannah, it's you!" It's the Young Man from Wednesday night and he's partially lucid, and partially out of his mind. For better or worse, he's a lot like me with an outsized sense of himself he can't hide for the sake of fitting into social norms. He vibrates on a higher frequency and when he speaks his mind, he sounds crazy to most people, even to me. I allow him to exist like this without judgment, a trait that gives most people a sense of comfort when they show up as their authentic self. In this freedom from expectation, we walk and talk for hours. When the conversation becomes serious about the situation with Couch Guy, he tunes in and becomes instantly lucid, long enough for me to tell him what was going on the night when we first met.

Through our conversation, I learn he's not 19 like his roommate, he's 28. And, neither one of them are gay. Furthermore, I learn that the apartment is not under renovation, is rented out to the 19-year-old son of Couch Guy's personal assistant/former girlfriend. He is being evicted at the end of October, along with the Young Man and Couch Guy. In desperation, after being abandoned in Hawaii in July, Couch Guy agrees to pay her $50 a day to stay there with her son and sleep on his couch. As the story unfolds, and the role of his personal assistant becomes clear, the Young Man offers me her phone number so I can connect with her.

Before I send a message, I need to go look at a short-term rental. The Young Man walks with me, and I ask him to wait outside for me while I look at the space. He leaves a poor impression with the man showing the apartment, but later in the month, the man offers me the space anyway. By then, I already have a place where

I can stay until I need to leave for the mainland in December, so I decline and he invites me out on a date, which I also decline. He's not my type, and now, I am really glad I found other accommodations.

When I come downstairs from viewing the apartment, the Young Man is gone, so I start to walk back to my AirBnB while I message other apartment listings to find a better place. The high rise where my current room is situated isn't ideal. It's an ok room in a former hotel that's been converted to personal residences, but there is no kitchen and the air conditioner smells musty. There's a great view of Diamond Head but no lanai. I want to find something more home-like with open air spaces. While I walk back to my room, I also send the personal assistant and his ex-wife, whose Instagram I've known about for a while, a brief message apologizing for leaving him here back in July, since his presence in the islands clearly causes more problems for more women, including the both of them.

The result is an hours-long conversation where I learn that his personal assistant is just another ex-girlfriend, who pre-dates his ex-wife. She is the one who flew him to Honolulu in July and she's the one who rents the black Nissan he is driving when he picks me up from the airport in October. He convinces her to do this after he takes her, in her own car, on an evening of DoorDashing to prove he can pay for the rental car, and the $50 a night to sleep on the couch in her son's apartment in Waikiki. In the apartment next door to the building where he finds his new girlfriend.

The personal assistant's contributions to the puzzle only solidify the notion that every word he's ever spoken is a lie. He owes her more than $80,000 and counting, as she continues to incur expenses related to the rental cars she recently arranged for him–unpaid parking tickets and vehicle damage. And he hasn't been paid the agreed upon $50 per day for the couch and the car.

While we finish up our conversation, I receive dozens of messages from his ex-wife telling me about how he hasn't seen his daughter in 11 years, and how far behind he is on child support and alimony. He also owes her more than $100,000. She hasn't had him served in recent years because she doesn't know where he lives. I give her the address where he stays with his new girlfriend.

I spend the rest of that day making arrangements to see various apartments and, in early afternoon, I drive up to a Wa'ahila Ridge State Recreational Area to play a casual round of disc golf. It turns into a mess with one of the local players turning a rabidly drunken assault at me for reasons no one quite understands. It is the first time I ever think I will have to fight someone on the disc golf course. It is wildly upsetting, especially since, until that moment, everyone was having a really good time. I am truly devastated, and with more anger in my heart than I care for, I leave and go back to my AirBnB in tears.

In the early evening, I brush myself off and I take another walk to Waikiki where I sit on that same bench and watch the sunset while I make arrangements to see more places the next day. I revisit that bench frequently. It's across the street from the hotel where we stay when we first came to Hawaii in July. While I am in downtown Waikiki, I see so many beautiful people.

Everywhere I look, there are gorgeous men, lovely couples, beautiful groups of happy vacationers, and I turn up my frequency so I can be seen, and perhaps absorb this radiant joy. I need to cleanse myself of the drama that seems to be accumulating around me. There's a handsome man on a green moped I see at a food cart on my walk back to my room. We saw each other briefly earlier in the evening and wave at each other but he doesn't try to talk to me either time. Back in the cool of my air-conditioned room, I fall asleep scrolling through apartment listings and compulsively swiping on men in the dating apps.

The next day, I get up early, but not quite as early as the day before, and still end up heading out for coffee before the sun rises. I revisit the bench in Waikiki and while I sit there watching the waves and the surfers, I realize I need to file a police report about what's been happening with Couch Guy, if for no other reason than to create documentation for his current girlfriend, who I want to help, despite her feelings of betrayal.

She thinks I'm being vindictive, even though she knows he owes me $15,000 and even after she comes to know he owes all of his ex-girlfriends and ex-wife substantially larger sums of money, she still thinks the problem is me. If not now, eventually, she'll come to accept the whole truth and the documentation may be helpful. I get off the bench and walk over to the police station which is just a half block down the beach and finish my coffee with an officer.

I start by telling him "I want to tell a story." Some, or all of it, may involve criminal behavior, and ask if he can provide some guidance around any portions of the story that might be worthy of additional investigation. I spill what I can without overtelling the details that aren't necessarily worthy of their attention, with a focus on the unpaid landlord, and I deviate briefly to the situation when he took my car to Michigan and used my AmEx without my consent.

It's this last detail where they advise me the charges to my card that are over $300 qualify as felonies, if they occurred in the last six months. The police report leaves out everything that isn't related to those charges, and I walk away from the station feeling like I did the right thing. I make a follow up phone call to the police in Michigan and the community probation office where he's under supervision for the DUI charges earlier in the year and I learn he now has a felony warrant out for his arrest there.

He's been bragging to anyone who will listen that the community probation officer has known him since childhood and is falsifying his reports to make it appear like he is complying with the no-drink order on the terms of his bail–he's out of jail still awaiting trail for the January DUI. They issue the warrant when he fails to appear. If I had let the police do their work when we first encounter them outside 'his' building on Wednesday after the comedy club fiasco, he would have been arrested on that warrant. If I had known then what I know now, only 48-hours later, I would have let them.

CHAPTER 16

HAWAII, ON MY OWN TERMS

On my way back to my hotel, I see the man on the green moped again and light up my frequency to make sure he sees me. When we make eye contact, I raise my eyebrows, stick out my tongue, and flash him a peace sign. He makes a rapid left turn and I already know he's coming around the block, so I linger at the next intersection where I expect him to emerge looking for me. He gets off his moped and greets me with a hug and kiss and tells me his name. He is on his way to the farm market nearby but first wants to know if my plans for the afternoon involve him. When I tell him I plan to spend the day looking at potential rentals, he offers to show me around town and orient me to various neighborhoods I might enjoy, as long as I can wait for him to get his produce.

We agree to meet at a local mall that is convenient to his home after he finishes at the market so I can follow him there. He parks his moped, puts away his groceries, and says his noontime prayers before we head out into the city. After a few hours of exploration, where he shows me all the best neighborhoods, we decide to get food before we call it a night.

We find a place and get on the waitlist but after thirty minutes, we are both over the wait and hungrier than we thought, so we decide to leave and find a Thai place where we order takeout instead. We visit a neighboring organic grocery store while we wait for our food and get fresh pressed juice to go with our meal. He tests me by suggesting I should pay as a sign of gratitude for his time.

Fresh pressed juice is expensive, even in Hawaii where the tropical fruits grow, but I still pull out my card to pay. He's not wrong about gratitude. I truly am grateful, and perhaps a little hopeful that meeting someone randomly like this, rather than on an app, may result in an actual relationship–which is always on my mind as a possible outcome. Even after all the drama with Couch Guy, I seem to be seeking a partner, or at least the validation and visibility of being desired.

When we get to his place, his landlord is on the couch reading. She and I chat briefly while he sets the table with plates and pours us tall glasses of juice to go with the curry and naan we picked up. Our brief conversation reminds me that AirBnBs in Honolulu now require a minimum 30-day stay, and there is pending legislation for 90-day stays, which is shifting an already volatile market for rentals. Especially short-term rentals, which is what I need since I plan to stay in Hawaii into December and return to the mainland before my son's birthday mid-month. It's not until the next day when I find myself flustered by the rental landscape on marketplace, and think back to this evening, that it occurs to me that I should check AirBnB for possible options with longer rental periods.

With my house back on the market, and reimbursement from Couch Guy now clearly an impossibility, I can't sign a long-term lease. Before leaving for Hawaii, I promise my son I will come back to the mainland for his birthday in mid-December, and I tell both the kids that I will try to bring them to Hawaii for Christmas if things work out as planned. It's rapidly approaching Halloween, and things are clearly not working out as planned, so I'm realistically only able to stay another five or six weeks if I want to honor that first promise, the one I made to my son.

When we are just about to sit down to eat the Thai food we brought back to his place, Mr. Moped reminds me to first wash my hands, which I do at the kitchen sink and then sit next to him while we eat and talk through a strategy for finding me a short-term place. When the dishes are washed and the leftovers are put away, we go up to his room and I stretch out on his bed while he steps away briefly for evening prayers. When he returns, he informs me we are taking a shower, so I follow him to the bathroom, which has square, tile shower that is halfway outdoors with living plants integrated to the exterior wall/window opening from the backyard garden. It's paradise. It's Hawaii.

We shower together and he steps out, over the very tall, ceramic tile tub wall, into the bathroom before I finish. When I step out, he hands me a clean towel and we walk back to his room. He has poured a small bowl of raw, liquid coconut oil into a bowl which he brings into the bedroom and casually places next to the bed. I don't really notice it until it comes into use a few minutes later, when, after discussing sex and deciding against it since neither of us has a condom, he asks for a hand job.

He instructs me to use the coconut oil generously, and frequently until he finishes. It doesn't take too long, but long enough for me to wonder what, if any pleasure I might receive in return, or if this is just another gratuity. When he's done, we return to the bathroom and shower again, and once more, he steps out before me and this time, I watch him as he wipes his ass repeatedly. Coconut oil clearly made its way down around his scrotum, across his perineum, and into his entire ass crack.

It would be comical if he weren't so serious about personal hygiene and cleanliness. He invites me to show myself out with a promise to see me again. We exchange a few messages over the next few weeks, and occasionally talk over FaceTime, but we don't reconnect until late November when he visits my AirBnB.

He comes by mid-afternoon, after work on a weekday. He brings a portable container of coconut oil. He wants another handjob, and he wants me to use anatomically correct terms to narrate our encounter. He promises he can go more than once, and then shows me a video of what he wants to do. It's a blonde woman on her knees, face up, mouth open, maneuvering herself to catch a man's explosive ejaculate. It's orchestrated pornography and nothing close to this scene has ever happened in any sort of real, authentic sexual encounter.

Still, I assure him we can try to recreate it, and I start with slow and gentle strokes to caress the head with gentle squeezes as he moves through my hands. When I say penis, he emits an audible sigh and his body contracts with pleasure. I am laughing on the inside because the seriousness of the correct terminology juxtaposed to the impossibly orchestrated cum shot is wildly funny to me.

Again, it doesn't take long, but long enough to wonder what pleasure I might get in return, what it will be like to have him inside of me–he's trim and fit, just barely taller than me, with the softest skin, and my body is hungry for his pleasure. When he finishes, he gets dressed and leaves without reciprocating in any way even though he had assured me he came prepared for more than one round and wants to go all the way with me since we both are prepared with condoms this time. I decline future offers.

The morning in October after our first encounter though, I have to check out of the temporary AirBnB I found when I left Couch Guy behind. I arrange to see a room in nearby Ewa Beach that I find on BLK when I mention the need to find a place to one of my matches and he happens to have a room available in his house. Before I check out of the AirBnB and leave for Ewa Beach, I spend a good deal of time scouring marketplace looking for other possible living arrangements.

Remembering the conversation with Mr. Moped's landlord, I open AirBnB to search there, thinking back to the previous evening and my brief conversation with Mr. Moped's landlord, and I find a handful of rooms that appear to be managed by two different hosts in two different neighborhoods. Between the changing regulations and high demand for housing on the island, there's a dearth of options. After looking at the two neighborhoods where I find the possible options, I reach out to one of them with questions about his rooms.

They look ok and they're advertised as being tied to a yoga studio which is in alignment with my goals–adequate rest, nutrition, exercise, connection–and it's super close to a beach. While I await his reply, I check out of the AirBnB and pile my stuff into the car and head out, first past the neighborhood where the AirBnB is located just to double check that it's not an unsafe area. Then I get on the highway towards Ewa Beach to see the room I found on BLK.

Ewa Beach is close enough to be considered part of the Honolulu metropolitan area, and like all other communities it isn't super far from the beach, but this place is not walkable. It's in a gated community that is sterile without any open greenspace, which seems unusual for Hawaii, and there's no easy access to anything really. He's very nice, and extremely handsome, but just shows me the room without making any moves, even though we met on a dating app. I let him know I'm not super keen on his place due to the geography, plus it is not furnished, but I'll give it some thought since I do need a place as soon as possible. It's not a good fit, and he's not either, but we remain connected on the dating apps and Snapchat, with occasional banter, but never a connection.

On my way back to Waikiki, I get a message from the AirBnB host with the yoga studio in his house. He has an apartment closer to Waikiki he can show me and if I don't like it, we can head over to his house in 'Aina Hina to look at his other room. I also get a message from a handsome man on BLK who wants to meet me for dinner at sunset. The studio is nice, but more than I want to spend for the time I have available in Hawaii, so we agree to move on to the house. He apparently does not have his car at the apartment, so he rides with me, giving directions and talking the whole way.

He tells me about his five-star reviews, the types of guests he's had over the years, how I can save money if I pay him directly instead of booking through the app, and that if I really want, I can pay for two nights and a key deposit just to see if I like staying there. He also tells me about his yoga studio aspirations, about the yoga studio down the street, and that he's an avid kite surfer who drinks strawberry-banana-mango-papaya smoothies twice a day instead of eating regular meals. He talks chaotically, with all this information intensely interspersed with driving directions and I cannot stop thinking about how this man's first name is the same as Couch Guy's last name.

After seeing signs that reminded me of my sister and my dad when I first arrive in Hawaii, and all the crazy things that happen immediately after that, I mull around if perhaps those signs were warnings that I somehow missed. Gentle reminders that I came to do the radically important work of grieving, and nothing else. I pull up into his driveway which is steeply angled, park behind his surfboard-laden SUV, and engage the parking brake before getting out of the car.

The house is in a very nice neighborhood, but it isn't well kept. He's making excuses for the condition before we get to the door, while also introducing me to his dog. He shows me where the washer and dryer are, in the breezeway between the garage and the house, to which the main door is permanently propped open. The only thing weirder than this AirBnB host are the rooms in his house. Directly inside the house is an area curtained off that is apparently one of the "rooms" and because of the open doorway, this particular room is an open-air room.

We slip our shoes off by the curtains and turn around to step into the house through another always-open doorway into a dinette and kitchen. There are two bedrooms and a bathroom off the dinette and a master suite off the hallway that leads to a living room with hardwood floors, which is the room being converted into a yoga studio. There is a table and chairs in the corner, yoga mats on the floor, and the front door is propped open with a brick. There is a locked wrought iron screen door, absent its screen. Opposite the front door is a lanai with a single lounge chair.

The curtain room is rented out for several months by a young woman who is a swim instructor, the host lives in the master suite, and the two other rooms are identical. He shows me the available room and tells me the other room is occupied by a woman from Japan. I agree to take the room for two nights and pay via Venmo but know I won't stay long since he doesn't allow renters to have guests at the house. He gives me the key and tells me where I can park the car after I bring my bags inside. Which I do, and then flop on the bed. It's too hot, so I turn on the air conditioner. It smells like mold, which confirms the need to look for better accommodations, but at least it's cold.

The bed is cheap and uncomfortable, and the linens are very old, but hopefully clean. There is a pile of clean, very old linens outside the bathroom door. It's an encouraging sign that the bed is at least clean. The bathroom is surface clean, but shabby, and the fixtures are tarnished with hard water buildup, but it will have to do for now. After a shower and a nap, I leave to meet my sunset date, Mr. Erickson.

Our timing is off, so we meet later than we expect, long after the sun already set. We end up at a different restaurant after we discover the first one is closed due to a water main break in that area. We agree to meet in front of a mall but I can't find him when I get to the entryway so I call him and describe the stores I can see in the immediate vicinity. He guides me to look in his direction where he appears from around the corner, and I can tell from afar that he is extremely fit.

He is almost bursting the thigh seams of his designer jeans and the buttons on his collared shirt are taught. From the very beginning he seems enthralled with me, holding my hand, looking deep into my eyes, and smiling through small talk while I drink iced coffee and he sips the beer and wine he orders for himself. We eat casually and when the bill comes, he pays and walks me to my car holding hands. He invites me to follow him to his apartment, even though it is kind of a mess he's already apologizing for.

We hug. He kisses me gently but passionately and I agree to his invite as I pull away to get in the car. He tells me I can park in his space when I arrive, and he texts me his address. I drive over to his apartment complex where he's waiting in the driveway to direct me to his parking spot. He opens my car door and offers me his hand as I step out of the car. We walk up to his third-floor apartment, all the while, he's holding my waist, grabbing my butt, and leaning in to steal kisses. It's adorable.

His apartment appears to be in a stage of disorder related to moving. There are empty boxes and half unpacked boxes around kitchen and living room. He tells me he just moved into the place in August and hasn't had time to completely unpack and set up even though it's already mid-October. It's stifling and there's no air conditioner running. The bedroom is humid and heavy with the smell of coco butter lotion, which I learn he uses to pleasure himself to sleep most nights. I slip out of my sundress in one swift motion.

Naked, I open the sliding door to the lanai and walk out into the night, enjoying the cool breeze and gazing out over the city. He doesn't seem overly concerned about the visibility, but the open door bothers him enough that when I come inside and stretch out on the bed, he gets up and closes it, cutting off the breeze from outside and condensing the hot scent of coco butter.

It's not uncommon for me to ask for a massage in these circumstances, and today is no exception. He opens a drawer next to the bed to get massage oil and it's full of toys–collars, paddles, cuffs–he rolls the drawer closed after selecting an edible strawberry massage oil. The massage is disappointing in every way, except the ending, which is quite happy. A few minutes of random, heavy pressure and stroking with his forearms across my thighs quickly yields to licking, touching, kissing, and eventually sex.

The fitness isn't an illusion, he has washboard abs, broad shoulders with huge biceps, rigid thighs, and like a lot of other short men I encounter, he's extremely well endowed. He knows it, too. After the brief massage, he devours me. He knows I need to be primed to receive his massive girth. He moves upward to face me, and he tries to move the right-hand ring I wear, a diamond solitaire, to my left hand. He wants to enact a wife fantasy. The heat and humidity have my fingers swollen too much for an easy transfer, so I tell him to forget about it and we keep going, hot and heavy.

When we take a break, I get up on walk onto the lanai for some fresh, cool air. He farts loudly, which I ignore, and when I come back in the room it stinks. I'm disappointed when he gets up to shut the door again. We reconvene in the bed and before long I am encouraging him to wrap it up. What starts as intense, if not contrived, lovemaking has devolved into mindless thrusting as he closes his eyes and takes himself elsewhere in his mind to finish. It takes another 10 long minutes. When he's done, I get up, slip into my sundress, thank him for a lovely evening and head back to this gross AirBnB.

CHAPTER 17

PARADISE ON A BUDGET

In the morning, I send a note to another AirBnB host who explains he has a room that is open through December 6 if I can wait one more day to check in. I drive by the house and decide I like it, and the neighborhood, so I send the booking request and make arrangements to move from this rather unclean and unkempt AirBnB in ʻAina Haina into what is advertised as "Paradise on a Budget."

It's in a neighborhood within walking distance of Waikiki and reportedly has very clean bathrooms. That evening though, I have been invited out to meet another man I connect with on BLK. So, rather than rest I take advantage of having a rental car and head out to meet a very handsome man my own age.

He wants to make me dinner and sends me his address. I drive to the west side and up into the hills where he owns a large home and lives alone, with enough room for his kids when they visit. He's tall, broad, muscular, and slightly knock-kneed because of his height. He's kind in his interactions and a great conversationalist.

He casually prepares a meal of sweet potatoes and grilled steaks, and while he cooks, we talk about the beaches he likes to visit, which includes Polo, a well-known nude beach on the north shore. By the time he's plating our meals, we are both completely naked. We dine in the nude. He gives me his robe to wear out onto the deck where we smoke, and he has an after-dinner drink before he takes me to bed. We spend the night making love, over and over again, once in our sleep.

When we wake up early in the morning, we both have things we need to do, so we fall into what feels like a comfortable morning routine with showers and toothbrushing. He makes me a cup of coffee in his Keurig, and we chat a little before I head back to the dingy AirBnB for one last night before I transition to Paradise on a Budget.

Before I go, he agrees to help me out when the rental car is due at the airport. Only a few hours after I check into Paradise on a Budget, I return the car and he picks me up and takes me back to the new AirBnB where I spend the rest of my stay. He doesn't have time for anything more. Despite a smattering of messages between us, we struggle to reconnect. I never see him again.

❖❖❖❖❖

The new place is a total relief. After bouncing around from chaos to a temporary AirBnB, to the rather undesirable yoga studio AirBnB, which is frankly unlivable, the comfortable bed with clean linens, new towels, and an air conditioner that doesn't stink like mold, is a welcome landing spot. The bathroom is spotless, as promised in the listing, and I am exceedingly grateful.

Within a few days of settling into the new spot, I feel at home and recommence writing this book, and navigating my way into a new life. The AirBnB offers a private room with full access to the living areas, including an open-air lanai. Empty during the daytime and bustling in the evening with a rotating cast of characters–host, house boy, personal friends, guests, former guests–the lanai quickly becomes my preferred space to work and relax. There are themed parties planned for Halloween and Thanksgiving. It is instant peace, on a Wednesday, 11 days after arriving on island.

The next day, I report to Ft. DeRussey Recreation Complex in Waikiki at noon for what I'm told is a weekly, very casual disc golf round. In the aftermath of the disc golf fiasco the previous week, many members in the local community reach out to apologize and ensure me, what happened earlier will never happen again and isn't the norm for their local crew. Most of the people who show up on this day weren't even there, but everyone knows what happened, and they seem to appreciate the fallout of the encounter. Their rogue member shows up with an apology and hug, and and a whole new attitude towards everything and everyone after the feedback he received from his outburst the previous week. Everyone is happy to see me on the course, even him. Over the course of play on this Thursday afternoon, I settle into the local disc golf family. We go on to play on a weekly basis on this amazing, pop-up course where I'm now one of the locals.

I also leave that first round with a spot reserved the following Monday on a tour of the island's beaches with a local guide, who also happens to play disc golf. The tour is amazing with stops on the North Shore at Pipeline and Waimea Bay. We go stand-up paddle boarding in Haleiwa, where I am fortunate enough to jump off the bridge.

The guide also gives me several key pieces of advice for enjoying Oahu like a local, including where to rent a surfboard in Waikiki, and where along the beach a couple of novice surfers can teach themselves how to surf without overpaying for lessons. He says the best way to learn to surf is to find a friend who also doesn't surf and take turns pushing each other into the waves from the shallow sandbar in front of the pink hotel–The Royal Hawaiian. He also recommends several waterfall hikes, and like many other locals, raves about international travels in Bali, Thailand, South Korea, Australia, and other far-flung places that rekindles the possibility thinking.

Travel is never far from my mind, and the possibility to travel more adventurous places opens up to my imagination in Hawaii.

Later in the evening after the tour, in the lanai at Paradise on a Budget, a conversation emerges between me and one of the people who is visiting the host. Kyle, to whom this book is dedicated, used to live in the same town as me–weirdly random–at the same time as me. We find it interesting that we are meeting for the first time on a lanai in Honolulu.

When the host asks about my day, and I relay what I learned about surfing, Kyle mentions that he doesn't surf and definitely wants to meet up with me to try. We exchange contact information and two of us end up spending most of our Sundays over the rest of my stay learning to surf, eating açaí bowls, smoking joints, and discussing philosophy. We discover we are the same person, mirrors of each other, and rapidly become the best of friends–platonic friends, which I desperately need, even more than I need or want a new life partner. Apparently, I need and want genuine and deep non-sexual connections with people on my wavelength. Later in my room, I spend some time swiping on profiles and chatting with matches as I settle in to sleep for the night, happy to have met someone I can learn to surf with.

Before anymore of these matches seize the opportunity to meet me in real life, Mr. Erickson already wants to take me out again, and I agree to a Friday night date. He wants to pick me up and take me to a comedy club for the late show. He shows up in a shitbox car that I assume is an island runner, so I slide into the shabby seat without judgement. In retrospect, it is really more of an indicator that he's an illusion rather than a high-value partner prospect. The designer clothes overlay cheap, dingy undergarments. His apartment is cheap, with no air conditioner, and eventually, I learn he has bad credit, too. He's an enjoyable FWB, but not a life partner, so with that perspective, I always enjoy a good time with him and indulge his fantasies but never really consider him more than a friends with benefits.

It's a Halloween themed show at a local club that he's been wanting to check out. Without asking which club, I agree to the date knowing he may take me to the club where Couch Guy (and I) reportedly own the VIP seating. When we pull up to the place on Friday evening, I laugh audibly at the prospect we may encounter him when I see the name of the club. It's the same place, and the owners of the club are among the people Couch Guy suggests he will connect me to as part of my soft landing in Honolulu, so I already know their names.

Mr. Erickson tells me that he considered purchasing VIP seating ahead of our date but decided to wait and purchase tickets at the door after reading up on the venue. He pays the $25 cover charge for each of us, and we go inside to find a seat. The club is literally just five rows of chairs with five seats on each side of the aisle.

There's a small coffee table in each row. There is no stage, just a mic under hot lights, with a pair of couches on either side that serve as the VIP seats. The bar, where Couch Guy suggests I can take occasional shifts to earn extra money, is actually a folding table in a mop closet at the back of the room with an ancient cash register and a few bottles for mixing drinks. There's a cooler for beer and a few wine selections. I opt for water since I can't drink any of the mixers and they don't serve coffee.

The show is actually very funny, and more interactive than typical comedy shows, mostly because there are exactly seven people in the audience besides me and Mr. Erickson. On the way out, Mr. Erickson stops to talk with the club owner, who I address by name, "you must be Christy" to which she agrees and thinks perhaps we have previously exchanged emails. As we awkwardly shake hands, I assure her, we have not met by email or any other way, but I know her name all the same, because I know things, and I leave it at that. I just smile sweetly while Mr. Erickson takes photos for his social media feed and when we depart the comedy club, I burst into joyful laughter.

Mr. Erickson does not know the backstory, so on the way back to Paradise on a Budget, I tell him the story of how Couch Guy came to owe me $15,000 and how I came to be in Hawaii both because of him and in spite (or perhaps despite, or to spite) him. As it turns out, this isn't the only time Mr. Erickson takes me somewhere that overlaps the Couch Guy experience. A sunset dinner in early December brings us to House Without a Key–one of the restaurants Couch Guy claims to have worked in when he previously lived in Hawaii before the pandemic. It's the same one he brings me to see on our failed July vacation in an attempt to build credibility and establish trust by showing me the places he used to know.

Back at Paradise on a Budget, Mr. Erickson and I head upstairs to room number two, my room. We ignore the gathering on the lanai, and proceed to link, rather quickly this time since it's late. Afterwards, we sit on the lanai to socialize, but he just falls asleep trying to snuggle with me, which is awkward in the otherwise lively and talkative scene. I nudge him awake and send him home so I can retire back to my room and recommence conversations with several promising future dates: Mr. Maui, Mr. Motorcycle, the Electrician, the Lego Man, and the Foodi are all keen on meeting in real life. I insist they make plans to do something, anything. It need not be elaborate or expensive, but I am not meeting up with someone to link if we can't also go do something first.

Mr. Maui, as his name implies, lives on another island and insists I come visit him. Eventually, I agree to a weekend trip to meet him in real life if he pays for the flight. We have a constant flow of conversation that leads up to the trip in early-November, but I am still meeting local men in Honolulu and tourists in Waikiki in the days before that trip. The day after the comedy club date, the Foodi offers to take me to a series of botanical gardens and temples on the west side of the island. He picks me up from the AirBnB to spend the day exploring, we stop for smoothie bowls, and then head over to his apartment as the sun is setting. His house is in disarray, because like all the military men on the island, his belongings just arrived from some far-flung locale and he hasn't yet unpacked. Notwithstanding, his home is orderly and clean, and he has two beds–the result of months-long delays in receiving his household goods, during he had to duplicate several key household items to survive, including his bed and his Ninja Foodi, of which he now has three in his kitchen.

We link and it's over too soon. His body is perfectly chiseled without a trace of fat, and he's not anywhere close to the 5'4" he claims on his profile. He's self-conscious about being only 5-feet tall. His light brown skin belies his Caribbean roots. As it turns out, I like Black men, of all shades, and find those with intersecting identities to be my favorite–island men, African men, magical men. I'm not sure why I like these specific types of men. I'm not looking for them on purpose. I just know that when I meet someone I like enough to get to know, it's common for them to be immigrants, or have parents who are, and come either from Africa or the Caribbean.

We talk about the struggles for short men in the dating scene, and how he enjoys being with me since his height doesn't concern me in the least. Our conversations flow naturally, and he feels a sense of calm and comfort he finds pleasant. When he gets up to shower, I hope for another round, but he dresses instead to indicate he is ready to take me back to my place down in Honolulu. His Waipahu apartment is at least a 30-minute drive even when there's no traffic.

On the way, we talk about seeing each other again, and agree that future adventures are in order. When he drops me off, he lets me know he'll reach out again soon, and true to his word, we end up on sunset beaches, with happy endings in my room at the AirBnB on several occasions during my fall stay at Paradise on a Budget. My current tenure in Hawaii is defined by the availability of room number two, through early December, and he makes sure to see me often, right up to the last weekend.

Seeing the Foodi for a Saturday of exploring temples and botanical gardens isn't the only date I make for the weekend. On Sunday, Lego Man arrives to pick me up early for an 8 am hike of Diamond Head. He's slightly overweight, with a barrel chest and quiet, polite demeanor. He laughs often when he's unsure what to say next and appears nervous but manages to hold a decent conversation. We make our way up and through the pathways and stairs of the former military installation engaged in small talk.

He arranges reservations online in advance of our arrival, which I appreciate since making plans is a tall order for most of the men I encounter on the apps. I learn he's another military man with a job he can't really discuss, so we find other topics of conversation. The hike is awesome with breathtaking views of the ocean and Oahu's shoreline all the way to Pearl Harbor. It's the first and only time I make the hike while I'm on the island.

We take a few photos along the way and after enjoying some time at the peak of the crater, we proceed back down to the car by passing through the bunker and down the spiral staircase to a long tunnel of steps that lead back to a tunnel along the trail. We stop for coffee before he brings me back to the AirBnB where he drops me off with a hug and gentle kiss on the cheek–it is an actual date and I enjoy it enough that we make weekly plans to meet up for a new hikes on Mondays while I'm on island.

It isn't until we have met for three hikes that he kisses me on the lips when he brings me home. Later in the evening after that first real kiss, Lego Man suggests he wants to meet with the intention to link and asks me if I will spend the night with him at his house. I agree and let him know he can make plans with me when he's available. He doesn't reach out to firm up a date until after Thanksgiving when I have just two weeks left before I'm scheduled to leave for the mainland. Before Lego Man and I have the chance to get out on those additional hikes or make plans to link, Mr. Motorcycle shows up, as planned. It's Monday, the day after the first hike at Diamond Head with Lego Man.

❖❖❖❖❖

Mr. Motorcycle really wants to meet me even though I am substantially older than his 28 years. I agree when he says he will take me on a waterfall hike recommended by the tour guide as an easy, close hike worth the effort for anyone seeking to avoid tourist traps. He offers me his helmet and we ride up into the rainforest to hike Manoa Falls. After we make it all the way to the falls, we take a side trail in an attempt to get to the top of the falls. It's impassable after 20 minutes, so we stop to rest with casual caresses that become passionate kisses. We stop and turn back when another pair of hikers comes upon the closed segment of the trail. They unknowingly interrupt what is surely about to become to outdoor sex.

I grasp onto his hips as he maneuvers his motorcycle back to the AirBnB, sure that he intends on coming upstairs with me, but when we arrive, he drops me off with a hug and a kiss, and a promise to come back later that evening. He has family in town, so he has to go home. He dons his helmet, takes off, and doesn't return, leaving me wondering if he might be one of those rare matches who just really isn't into me after meeting in real life. A day or two later though, he reaches out with an apology and an offer to meet up the following Monday since it's once again his day off. He wants to know if I would consider accompanying him to a well-known nude beach on the North Shore, to which I agree. We call it a date.

The conversation with Mr. Maui continues to be pleasant and polite. He hasn't sent me a dick pic yet, and he's moved from the Facebook dating platform to my Facebook page and the messenger platform. We close in on our travel plans and I send him my travel information so he can book the flight a week in advance. I am immediately on my way out the door for another date with Mr. Erickson after our travel plans are confirmed. We head out for dinner almost every week, and on this occasion, he shows up with a collar, paddle, and lingerie so we can cultivate more creative and in-depth encounter before dinner. We take photos and video, some featuring just me, and some featuring both of us. It results in extremely erotic content and a hot link that fizzles towards the end as he turns inward to finish with heavy and hard thrusts that last too long when I ask him to wrap it up.

We clean up a little after and head out for Thai food at a neighborhood hotspot. He drops me off with a hug and kiss and suggests a sunset at China Walls later in the week. We make the date but miss the sunset since he shows up later than expected after negotiating Honolulu's notoriously bad rush hour traffic. We still manage to catch a colorful sky at a restaurant in Hawaii Kai which is close but we never make it out to China Walls. We skip the link afterwards, at my request, since he's extremely well endowed and I haven't yet recovered from our last encounter. I can barely manage to link with average sized partners right now. There's no way I can go again with him so soon after our last encounter.

As a compulsive swiper, I continue to match with men on the dating apps, even when I'm maxed out and needing a break from Mr. Erickson, and one in particular has my attention. Mr. Big is very tall, extremely handsome, and he has his act together with a great career. When I suggest meeting for dinner, he sends me his phone number and aside from exchanging a few text messages, he also calls me via FaceTime. He sends an invite to dinner via OpenTable the following day. It's a sushi restaurant so I review the menu and immediately know there's not much I can, or want, to eat. But, in the spirit of trying new things, I don't complain. After an appetizer of fried shrimp, we share a huge plate of raw fish. He eats far more of it than I do, but I try a few of the varieties after he shows me how people typically eat these kinds of dishes with wasabi and soy sauce. It's not my favorite and he knows.

We exchange a few stories over dinner, and I learn he's been burned by his former wife. I can see it in his face when he thinks about his marriage that he's still hurting from its dissolution. Perhaps it's a mirror. Somehow, the story about Couch Guy spills out, even though I realize I need to stop thinking about it, talking about it. I need to just get over it. And I definitely need to stop telling potential romantic interests, especially the ones I might want to take seriously.

He is instantly hooked and wants to hear the whole story. Then he asks to hear more stories. I tell him I am writing a book–this book–about my experiences in the dating apps, dating during the pandemic, and dating after divorce. I explain that I spend my days in the lanai at the AirBnB weaving these stories together with the fabric of my life since the divorce. After dinner, we head back to Paradise on a Budget where I offer to show him the lanai. It's empty on this evening, and we pass by on the way to room number two without dwelling. He didn't come to see the lanai and we both know it.

The link is electric and explosive–he unlocks all my levels, and despite his lack of chiseled abs, his body is nothing but desire. I always like tall, broad men–the kind who make me feel tiny. Throughout this story, I link with a wide variety of men with different body types. The athletes and fitness models hold so much appeal, especially when they show up with swagger, and offer validation. They tell me they want me, need me, even, and how much they love my body, that my pussy feels so good. I secretly enjoy it when they can't last very long. It underscores their raw desire for me.

Mr. Big shows up with confidence and presence enough to capture my full attention though. His 6'4" frame feels intensely larger than mine, with muscles that suggest he was once a hot, young body with chiseled abs. He's my age now, and still muscular and strong with softness in his midsection. A gold chain with an eagle-globe-anchor pendant hangs around his neck and tickles my cheeks when he holds me close. His smooth skin smells so good, and his firm grip, passionate kisses, and gentle wordless domination leave me weak with desire. When he's finished, he showers and redresses without toweling off.

Afterward, he asks me why I don't do my work in a different context to enrich myself. He's seen programs where I can apply my skills to get money for myself and he sends me a website for a training provider who's lauded in my line of work as a scourge on our profession. It's laughable, actually. My coworkers would hold an intervention if they thought I was hanging out with someone who took this seriously. I ignore the advice and focus on the quality interaction that just happened. We end up meeting for dinner on a few other occasions, and more than once, we just meet at Paradise on a Budget–a true afternoon delight.

We talk about spending more time together after a few enjoyable dates, perhaps spend an afternoon in his apartment playing house–cooking, dining, lovemaking, falling asleep in each other's arms. He loves the idea but when I push for a time we can do this before I leave, he tells me he is going to be busy traveling for Thanksgiving. He suggests perhaps we can play house when he gets back at the end of the month. I like him more than I should, and when I tell him I want to be greedy with his time in that last week before I leave in early December, he pushes me away with cruel words. I delete his contact information and forget about him a week before I leave the island, chalking it up to a reinforcement of lesson already learned: feelings are gross. I don't block his number though, I just forget about him, because I know, like all the other fuck boys I meet, he's not done with me. He won't be able to forget about me. So, as expected, a couple of weeks later, he offers an olive branch and apology. I am already back on the mainland for my son's birthday and Christmas.

After that first date with Mr. Big though, I have firm plans to visit Mr. Maui that include a plane ticket and the assurance of a ride at the airport, meals, and a place to sleep for the few nights I'll be staying there. I arrange an Uber to take me to the airport and Mr. Big agrees to pick me up when I land back in Honolulu on Saturday just a week after we first met for sushi. Before I fly out though, there's that nude beach date on my schedule and I meet another handsome young man on the dating app who wants to meet in real life. It's chaotic with dates almost every day. I am trying to actually meet someone, but I am also serial dating with multiple casual links because I never really meet anyone who's qualified for more.

Mr. Motorcycle shows up mid-morning to pick me up in a nice white sedan, which is his everyday car when the motorcycle isn't practical. The ride to the nude beach on the north shore is further than either of us want to make tandem on his motorcycle. The beach is casual and quiet when we arrive. It's before noon on a Monday, so there isn't a crowd, but the beach is full by the time we leave a few hours later. We spend the peak of the day basking in the sun and swimming in the ocean, often facing each other in casual conversation as the sun warms us, even through the intermittent shade cast by rustling trees along the back side of the sandy beach. The naked breeze feels good across my sun-kissed cheeks as the day wears on, and a slight grin comes across Mr. Motorcycle's face.

At first, I think it's me, and then he nudges me to look the other way where a nearby beach goer is casually working their way through sun salutations–in the nude. I shrug it off as normal for a nude back and draw his attention back to me. Before long, we are both distracted with the yoga man's antics. He's doing handstands and dolphin dives in the ocean directly in our shared line of sight. We are trying to be respectful and ignore him, but he's in waist deep water, upside down with his whole situation overly exposed.

The giggles take over and we decide to pack up and head back into Honolulu. When we get to Paradise on a Budget, I am not sure what to expect, but he comes inside this time. We link and it's hot, and we are both thirsty for more, but also in need of a shower to get the salt off our bodies. He says he needs to run home anyway, so he leaves with a promise to be back later in the evening, and just like last time, I don't hear from him again for a few days. It comes with an apology, and despite our efforts we only find one more opportunity to connect, right before I leave in December, and just like the other times we connect, we link and he's gone, with a promise to return that he has no intention of honoring–an annoyance that is reminiscent of Mr. Massage.

❖❖❖❖❖

The next day, The Electrician messages me asking if we can connect to smoke some herb and link, and initially, I decline. I don't want to walk the distance from Paradise on a Budget to his apartment on the Ala Wai Boulevard, which is on the other side of the canal. I agree when he offers to pick me up and bring me back, so I send him the address. When he picks me up, he tells me he's been to the lanai before to socialize with one of his coworkers who knows the host. Funny, small little world.

The ride around the canal is short and before long we are naked in his bed, breathless, and ready to go again. He's a big fan of spanking my cheeks, and I can feel the sunburn from the nude beach the day before. We take a few photos during our encounter that showcase my pink cheeks in stark contrast to his dark black skin, our bodies pressed together, his hand carefully but firmly grasping my throat, sly grins on both of our faces. He's vocal about how much he likes the skin color contrast, and especially how his hands look on my pink butt cheeks. I like it, too, I tell him as I watch us in the mirrored closet doors. It's an incredibly common dynamic with my links–they seem to appreciate the color contrast as part of their own fetishization of older white women.

He becomes a regular link with frequent encounters over the remainder of my stay in Hawaii. We text each other regularly and on several occasions our schedules align, so we find time to connect, even though he works constantly and even makes trips back and forth to the mainland. We enjoy each other's company, so sometimes we just hang out together, and our connection is one of those that grows over time to be what feels like a true friend with benefits situation.

Not for the first time, I sink into the notion that feelings might be ok, especially when the communication is easy and flowing, and expectations aren't clouding the air between us. He is devastatingly handsome, with characteristically good hygiene of a young Black man, that I always appreciate. He's playful with a gentle and understanding nature when we are deep in conversation, that's unlike his dominant alter ego that takes over when we link.

It's deeply appealing but this isn't likely to last. We are both heading back to the mainland before the new year with ambiguous plans to return. I'm aiming to be back early in 2023 and he's unsure when or how he'll return, and our respective mainland destinations are on opposite sides of the country. Still, we remain connected, exchanging messages frequently, and longing for another opportunity together.

CHAPTER 18

MAUI

With a roundtrip ticket booked from Honolulu to Kahului, I pack light for a couple of days exploring sunsets and beaches with Mr. Maui. I'm flying Hawaiian airlines and a slight departure delay means we watch the sunset in the car on the way back to his apartment rather than our planned beach rendezvous. It's a cute 1-bedroom lower apartment with a larger home above. There's a small backyard with papaya trees that slopes away from the house giving way to stunning ocean views beyond the beachside houses on the other side of his block.

He's unconventionally handsome, gentle, and mildly affectionate. He cooks a Cajun type shrimp dish with pasta and sets more food to marinate for future cooking while he casually moves through the kitchen preparing plates. The food is excellent and after we eat, we sit on the couch with the TV on as background noise while we explore each other's bodies. Passionate kissing giving way to close bodies and eruptive orgasms. We lay with each other on the couch for a while before I retire to his bedroom for the night. He stays up for a while longer and sleeps on the couch, even though I welcome him to join me in his bed. I don't like that. Part of the appeal for me is the opportunity to share a bed, to play house, if only for a few nights.

I'm up early the next morning to log a few hours of work before we head out from his place for an adventure–my leave recently expired so I am back to work at my remote IT job. He takes me for coffee around 6:30 am. When we get back to his place, he returns to the kitchen while I finish up work. Thanks to the time difference and my tendency to be up at 5 am, my work is finished, and we are able to hit the road before 10:30 am.

I don't know where we are going, but our first stop is back at Starbucks. Then we are off on the Road to Hana. We make several roadside stops for sightseeing, and more than once, he offers to take photos of families we see taking selfies. We stop for lunch at a country market, and he grabs himself a Cesar salad while I grab an açaí bowl and another cup of coffee. We get back in his car and he navigates to a vacation condominium spot where he assures me there is a public access point to the ocean.

We park in a small lot that is marked off for guests and he takes me along a pathway towards the water.

When we get there, we are on a rock outcropping that juts out into a little bay about 20 feet over the ocean. There is a small cove on the left that curves around to another point with a big open house perched up top. It looks like a couple of banquet servers are inside setting up for an event of some sort.

The house is an open-air structure with windows that fold open for full exposure, and it appears much older than the condos and vacation homes that have grown up around it. To the right of the point we are standing upon, there is another smaller cove that is open to the ocean which occasionally pushes a large surf surge up into the rocks, spraying our lunch spot with a light mist from the crashing waves.

There's a couple of other people here and they are jumping from the rocks into the larger cove on the left. It's protected from the open ocean by the point created by the rock outcropping where we are eating our lunch so there is very little wave action on that side. There's a Hawaiian Monk Seal sunning itself and occasionally diving down along the ledge where the cove opens up to the ocean, sea turtles are bobbing in the gentle surf along the inside of the point.

We finish eating and Mr. Maui pulls a beer from his grocery bag, drinks it, and then removes his shirt, hat, and shoes. He gets up from our spot, digs his wallet and keys from his pockets, stashing them in his grocery bag. He walks to the edge of the cliff on the left side and jumps in. He comes up in the pocket of the cove and returns to the top where a man and his son, who are visiting from California, start up a conversation about jumping. They are regular bridge jumpers in the Bay Area, often jumping 60 feet into coastal waters.

While they take turns jumping, I get up and move our spot to higher ground to avoid the increasing splash from the high surf coming from the little cove on the other side. Once I have us settled somewhere more protected, I take off my own shoes and sunglasses, and without a bathing suit since I didn't know this was on the agenda, I make the jump myself in my sundress. The sun is warm and so is the ocean. The jump is exhilarating! I climb out using the gentle rise of the surf in the protected cove to boost me up onto that first ledge. Then, I walk back up to the top like climbing steps, wringing the edges of my dress along the way, and observing a minor cut on my toe from the initial scramble out of the ocean.

When Mr. Maui sees me inspecting the cut, he pauses his conversation with the Californians to tell me I can call myself an official Cliff House jumper, since a little minor damage is the hallmark of jumping here. When he returns to his conversation, he resumes telling our new friends, who oddly jump in their shoes and without removing their tee shirts, that he's seen people jump from the high walkway on the other side of the smaller cove, and that he himself has jumped into the smaller cove from the rocks where we ate our lunch. In disbelief, they walk over to the other side and look down into the smaller cove. The ocean is choppier on this side, and occasionally, the surf comes in high and big waves crash into the rocks circling the cove. I can't hear the conversation, but I can see Mr. Maui talking and gesturing, in what I can only imagine is a description of how he reads the surf and only jumps if the conditions are just right. All of a sudden, he's gone. He jumped. And just as fast, he appears climbing over the edge back up onto the point.

In a mild panic, I move closer to make sure he's safe. I look earlier when he mentions that sometimes people jump that side and I know it's beyond my capabilities even in the best of conditions since I am unsure about the climb out. The jump I can manage, but I'm not big on rock climbing and I'm not trying to hurt myself, so I know I don't want to jump that side myself.

I can hear Mr. Maui now talking to the older of the two men–the dad–about how he timed his jump with the waves so he knew he would have enough time to get out and climb back up before a big wave came into the cove. We can see the waves breaking out in the distance and watch them approach the point and swell up into the cove, coming in sets of three, on a frequency of two or three minutes.

He jumps again in the lag between wave sets, and again, easily navigates back up to the top of the rock outcropping before another round of waves crash into the cove. At the top, the dad is standing in Mr. Maui's jump spot, contemplating his own jump. He watches the waves come and asks, "should I jump now?" Mr. Maui replies, telling him "No, I would have already jumped" and he raises his hand, pointing at the approaching surf but before he can explain further, the dad jumps, directly into a huge wave.

He is instantly distressed since the wave action is like a powerful washing machine throwing him against the rocks. He manages to get partially out, grabbing onto the rocks. I can't see him, but I can hear Mr. Maui coaching him to swing his legs up and out of the water, and then with more than a little panic, assuring him he'll be fine but needs to get higher up the rocks. He needs to climb, and fast. I am not sure exactly what happens next, but Mr. Maui has his hands on his head in a way that suggests he's very concerned about the dad, and then without a word, he scrambles down the cliff side and out of sight. The younger man–the son–follows and he's starting to shout, "help him, please help my dad, he can't swim." The wave action is intensifying, and they are gone from sight for too long, so I scurry over to the edge to look.

There are three faces in the water staring up at me in sheer terror. The older man is screaming for help, "someone please, help me, I don't want to die, I can't swim!" The younger man is just screaming "please help him, he can't swim." My friend, who is trying to help, is being submerged by the panicked swimmer in classic drowning fashion, as he tries desperately to keep his head above water by climbing his rescuer. It's a lesson we learn as lifeguards, never approach a distressed swimmer. Instead, this is why we offer them a floatation device from an arm's reach away.

With as much quickness as I can muster, I hurry back to our stuff and grab my phone to dial 911. The dispatcher answers and it sinks in–I am the caller that doesn't know where they are–and if my friend dies right now, I don't even know where he lives. I never made a note of the street name or house address.

I actually say it out loud to the dispatcher, "oh no, I don't really know where I am but there are people who might be drowning" and before she can ask me any more questions, I hear his voice in the back of mind *official Cliff House jumper* and I blurt it out, "I think I'm at a place called Cliff House" and I describe what I can see. She knows instantly where I am and assures me a rescue squad on jet skis is coming, but before they get there, she needs to know how many people and approximately where they are.

As I am on the phone describing the scene, a huge wave washes into the cove and slams the younger man, the son, up onto the rocks just below me about 10 feet away. He can get up and walk directly to me, but before he can respond to his situation, another giant wave washes up and grabs him, ripping him back into the ocean, which is 20 feet below when it isn't churning with surf. The older man, the dad, is still screaming for help in between waves that crash him into the rocks and then submerge him. My friend, Mr. Maui is now out in the open ocean. He dives down deep when the big wave comes crashing through and pushes himself off the rocks. He swims out of the cove where the surf is low, but the currents are fast. He's swimming but making no progress. The surf isn't huge outside of the cove, but the current is pulling him further from shore and away from the relative safety on the Cliff House side of the point.

Before the jet skis arrive, and while I am still on the phone with dispatch, a casual blonde headed surfer bro with chiseled abs and an instagram perfect girlfriend jumps into the smaller cove to help the older man, the dad. As a former lifeguard and generally smart individual, I know better than to get into that mess and I try to stop him. I chase after him pleading, "no, no, no, don't get in the water" but he ignores me and jumps in.

The dispatcher is listening, asking for details so she can relay the changing status to the jet ski rescuers. The surfer bro manages to get the old man out of the water and onto a ledge, coaxing him eventually all the way out onto the trail above the cove, taking an unconventional route, making incremental progress between crashing waves so he can rest between movements up the cliff face. He has the man tucked into crevices on the cliff, guarding him from the surf with his body as waves continue to batter the cove, moving slowly higher until he's safely on the trail.

The younger man, the son, who manages to get himself out of the surf twice, despite being slammed around violently by the waves, is periodically on shore shouting for help throughout the chaos. He draws the attention of workers in the Cliff House. One of them strips off his white, collared service shirt, grabs a surfboard, and paddles out into the ocean flooding me with a wave of relief. I know that the first person he is going to encounter is my friend. I am trying to watch everyone and communicate their status to the dispatcher when I see that the Cliff House employee finally reaches Mr. Maui–it's almost the same time as the surfer bro is dragging the older man out of the cove and onto the first ledge.

Everyone is safe, and the relief is palpable even to the dispatcher who starts asking me more pleasant questions and making sure that I stay on the line until everyone is on shore and assessed. The jet skis still come, and I can see them before everyone is safe, but they can't make it in time. Without bystander intervention, the old man 'will surely drown before they reach him and his son will certainly go in the water again, enduring more injuries until his dad is safe. He is bloody enough as it is so I'm confident that these bystanders saved lives. My friend may be able to float safely until rescuers arrive, and I loosely consider swimming out there myself before the surfer starts towards him. Relief is perhaps an understatement.

When I hang up, as soon as I know that my own friend is safely out of the water, I go find the older man to check if he needs first aid. He's still on the shoreline below in the relative safety of the cove on the left. He nods when I tell him I'll be right back.

While I am talking to the older man to make sure he's ok, his son finds his way over to the shady spot where his dad sat down to rest after being rescued. Since he comes up the other side of the cliff, it's a little way off from the jump spot. The dad seems ok, if not in a little bit of shock, and the son is bleeding profusely from a gash in his scalp and several scrapes and abrasions on his ribs, arms, and legs that come from being slammed into the rocks.

It doesn't occur to me to ask them why he was jumping into the ocean if he can't swim. I suggest they may want to seek medical care, and they assure me they will both be fine, so I leave them to return to my friend. I need to make sure he's going to be ok, too. Like so many others in this story, I never see them again, but I often wonder who they are and if they are ok.

Mr. Maui later tells me that while he is swimming in the open ocean, every time he looks up at me, I am further away. He starts to worry that he is becoming exhausted and may drown. He has no idea the Cliff House surfer is coming to help until he is right there offering him the board. He tries to send the surfer into the cove to help the man and his son, but the surfer refuses and insists he must first get him to shore, effectively saving him from exhaustion and drowning. Later, I write an email to the hospitality group that oversees Cliff House asking them to convey our gratitude to the employee who saved my friend. We never caught his name. As quickly as he appears in the ocean with his board, he returns to his work, without so much as word after bringing Mr. Maui to shore in the protected cove between the rock outcropping and the Cliff House.

My friend is banged up, with a few scrapes, bruises, and a deep abrasion on his tailbone. He throws up his lunch in a flood of beer and sea water and crawls into the shade where he naps for several hours before he feels well enough to drive us back to his house. The surfer bro who saves the older man is casually unfazed by the situation, writing it off with a shaka and "right place, right time" shrug of his broad, tan shoulders.

He and his girlfriend go on to jump the calm side for a while, making videos and taking selfies for their social media accounts. I watch them playing in the sun while my friend sleeps and they regard me with a sort of pity and reverence when they navigate over the vomit on their way to other adventures. They know I'm there with him, but completely unaware of the context. It's kind of a first date, kind of a hook-up, and in the end, turns into a one-night stand–we aren't a couple and I never see him again, either.

We drive in silence back to his apartment. I can tell he's managing significant pain in his ribs and his tailbone, where there is a scrape that is much more than skin deep. Discomfort and pain notwithstanding, he makes supper for us when we get back to his place, and we spend the evening in quiet conversation talking about what happened. He confesses a sense of responsibility for having jumped first and I assure him, it's not his fault. When it comes to water safety, personal responsibility for knowing your own limitations and capacities cannot be replaced. He didn't make that man jump, and if anything, was trying to explain the importance of reading the surf when the man jumped.

The fact that he jumped into the ocean when he clearly can't swim very well and is incapable of reading the surf, is entirely his own fault. If anything, my friend performed a commendable act when he attempts to save him, even though it almost cost him his own life. As it turns out, he was on the side of the cliff holding onto the old man by the wrist, trying to pull him up when the surf surged into the cove and washed them into the ocean. Before I head off to his bed alone, we agree that we want to revisit Cliff House to jump again and cleanse our palate of that wildly terrifying experience, but not on this visit. It still hasn't happened.

The next day, I wake up early, as always, and feel badly about asking him to take me for coffee, but he knows it's important to me, so we head over to Starbucks, and I grab a cup for my morning. Once we get moving, it's clear that he's still in considerable pain and any plans we have for the day are not happening. I'm scheduled to return to Honolulu after sunset, but I tell him he's welcome to drop me at the airport at any time since I'm flying Hawaiian and can surely get on one of their earlier flight options. At noontime, I have my bag packed and he drops me at the airport.

While I'm waiting to board, Mr. Connecticut starts a chat with me in Snapchat. I send him a cute selfie and tell him I need to be spoiled. He asks me how, so I tell him I want $50 for a pedicure, a request I make on occasion to other men, without much thought. They don't always say yes.

Sometimes I get no response, which is a response. Sometimes I get $50. Sometimes they laugh at me, and I don't really care. I just go get a pedicure and pay for it myself. But his response is wildly out of scope. He starts hurling rude insults at me that he's not a simp and not going to be paying my bills, which is inconsistent with the type of language he uses when he wants to convince me that our connection is unique, and wants me to talk dirty and send him graphic photos.

When he wants to get off, he says we should be together as a couple as soon as we meet in real life to confirm that we really like each other as much as we think we do. He tells me I am his dream woman and compliments me endlessly on my perfect appearance. He begs for nude photos, especially pictures of me with other men. He lusts after our shared kinks with elaborate fantasies centered around me and begs me to embellish them with my own dirty talk. But today, with this simple request to be spoiled, he angrily labels me a gold digger.

Maybe it's the trauma of what happened in the ocean, but suddenly, clearly, he's not a good match for me. He's being incredibly mean and petty over $50 that I don't even care about, and each and every response is couched so that he's a victim of me and my elaborate scheme to use him for his money, which he's saving to buy a house. Hey, it's a valid reason not to give someone $50 but his aggression is unacceptable, and I try to explain myself, but he just fires back with more insults. I block his phone number and delete him on SnapChat since I really do not need a love that tests me in any way.

Shared kink or not, he's being incredibly mean to me and I'm not allowing it. I was married to an incredibly mean person for 15 years and have no intention of dating someone who thinks they can just be mean to me. Without losing a step, he starts messaging me from a different number–probably his work phone–hurling more hurtful insults with more aggression that I can feel through the phone. I block the second number, track down and block all his social media, and board the plane stewing about this one.

For more than two years at this point, he's been in the back of my mind as a strong potential to be an actual partner, a man I can share my life (and kinks) with. But in the end, he's just another fuck boy. My earlier concerns that he is only texting me when he wants to jerk off is probably more accurate that I want to admit. He can say no in any number of fashions, but he doesn't need to be mean about it and he is clearly committed to misunderstanding my perspective. He isn't worth my time.

The flight is short, and Mr. Big is picking me up from the airport as planned. He likes my stories, so he asks about the trip, and I give him a short version of the near drowning events. He can tell I have something else brewing, so he asks what else is going on. Reluctantly, I relay the events that led me to first favor, and then cut off Mr. Connecticut. He's giggling a little and he shuffles around some things in his car and finds a few bills. He hands me $100 when I get out of the car and reminds me to upgrade to a deluxe pedicure and leave a good tip.

This is exactly the type of man I want in my life, but despite several appearances in this story, Mr. Big remains elusive. He can't be had, and secretly, I think he might have a wife or girlfriend that keeps him busy when he's ignoring me, and he uses my apartment and my body as a distraction from his real life. I've been the side piece so often at this point, I can recognize what's happening, even when no one is being honest with themselves about it.

CHAPTER 19

CHINA WALLS

After the chaotic encounter at Cliff House, the conversation with Mr. Maui continues. The first few days, it's really just me checking on him and his healing. He eventually heads to the doctor for what might be an infection in one of the abrasions on his leg, but a little self-care has the rest of his war wounds healing nicely. On Sunday, I recommend he find a second skin type bandage like the tattoo artists use to seal fresh ink and support clean healing for the tender, deep wound on his tailbone. Even though I know he's not relationship material, we keep up the conversation for a couple of weeks. He wants me to consider coming back to Maui instead of Oahu after the holidays.

The entire time I am in Maui, I ignore the dating apps, but do respond to a handful of text messages, including one from a New York City lawyer who uses a global feature to match with potential links in Hawaii in advance of a planned visit after Thanksgiving. After my early return on Saturday, I go for that pedicure and return to Paradise on a Budget to relax in the lanai and visit with the evening's cast of characters. I continue the chat with the visiting lawyer who arrived while I in Maui.

We arrange to meet on Sunday after Thanksgiving for sunset and decide to head to China Walls on the east side of the island since he has a rental car and I've heard it's a stellar sunset venue. He picks me up from Paradise on a Budget and we head east to Hawaii Kai and navigate to a neighborhood where we can park near the short trail that leads from a vacant cul de sac to the edge of the ocean. The trail takes us to a rock outcropping 20 feet above the ocean where dozens of locals are back flipping, twisting, and launching themselves into a gentle surf.

Occasionally, a big wave set rushes through, and everyone backs away from the edge with locals shouting to jumpers still in the water to back away from the rock face. A rescue jet ski is on patrol 100 feet out into the ocean, running back and forth along the length of the surf break. There's a sign above the rocks where hot bodies are strewn in the late afternoon sun, perhaps drying after their own jumps into the ocean. It advises people to use caution on the rocks, to listen to the local advice, and to be aware that the entire outcropping is prone to occasional battering by high surf.

The implication is that you can be washed away into the ocean, even from the flats when the conditions are right for big surf, but today, the biggest surf barely reaches the edge. Most of the wave action is small on this day, but I don't jump. I'm not dressed for it, not that I was wearing anything different earlier in the week when I jumped at Cliff House, but with that so fresh in my memory and a date who can't really swim at all, I opt to stay dry. After the sun goes behind the horizon, we return to the car and make the short drive back into Hawaii Kai to find supper. We eat a casual meal at the brewery–the same one Mr. Erickson took me to earlier that month when we missed the sunset–and then return to his friend's apartment in Honolulu. The link is both unremarkable and unique.

He's older than I am, and he's stout rather than fit, which often translates into a decent lover. It's like they try harder when they know they aren't on par with the type of man I usually match and link with. He's good for two rounds, which I appreciate even when it's of entire average quality. Afterwards, as we clean up and redress so he can bring me back to Paradise on a Budget, we chat a little about our professional lives and how our student loan debt governs somewhat unnecessarily, our professional trajectories–he's a public defender in NYC vying for public loan forgiveness. I'm locked into a career that facilitates my lifestyle, and pays the loans, rather than working as a public servant with an aim for loan forgiveness. I have seven of the 10 years required, but the pay differential in my line of work, between public and private employment, isn't worth it to me. Neither one of us is really winning when we work long hours more often than we relax on the beach.

We go into this encounter knowing full well it is just a link between two consenting adults, and I don't expect to hear from him again. What lingers in the morning is the taste of salt on my lips from dreams of my own leap at China Walls. I should have jumped while I was there, and I spend the next two weeks strategizing to get back there to jump before my scheduled return flight on December 6.

I set up a date with Mr. Motorcycle, who wants to jump and knows how to swim, but when that day rolls around, he comes over to link with me before my weekly Thursday disc golf round with a promise to pick me up afterwards for a sunset jump at China Walls. He predictably backs out an hour before he's supposed to pick me up.

Several others agree and fall through when they look online and see that the jump is largely considered to be dangerous, despite the regular presence of locals doing backflips when the conditions are right. When conditions aren't right for jumping, the locals can be found surfing the giant swells that run parallel to the elevated shoreline. Despite the near tragedy in Maui at Cliff House, I gain a taste for jumping when I first launch myself from the bridge in Haleiwa.

It's too late in the season to go back to Waimea Bay to jump the rock I skipped on my island tour, and I am still trying to get back there on a day when the conditions are right to redeem myself. As winter approaches, conditions at Waimea Bay deteriorate for jumping as the surf becomes dangerously high and a sand bar migrates into the jump zone but at the same time, the swells calm on the east side of the island and there isn't a better time to jump China Walls.

Despite only having a few days left on the island, I keep swiping and matching, and of course chattering with anyone who's consistent in my inbox. Most of the matches, both new and old, just want to link. Very few of them want to do anything that constitutes a date.

Fewer still are interested in jumping at China Walls with far too many matches claiming an inability to swim. In other circumstances, I would try to find something else to do with them, but my focus for the moment is on making the jump and there are no takers.

On Friday afternoon, I divert my focus to a lunch date with a non-swimmer only because he's leaving for the airport and won't be back until January. We meet for a late lunch, and he's surprised that I don't drive on the island but nonjudgemental when I explain my circumstances. We appreciate each other's company and, based on my assertion that I'll be back to Hawaii in the new year, agree to keep up the connection for future links. He's literally running out of time to make his flight when he drops me off at Paradise on a Budget, so the link simmers until an unlikely encounter on the mainland in the new year.

By Saturday though, with a return flight looming on Tuesday, I am losing patience with my matches and links who can't or won't jump with me. When I mention it to Kyle, he immediately agrees. We already have plans to surf the next morning. One last Sunday morning session before I head out. We have also already agreed to meet up Sunday evening for the Gay Men's Chorus of Honolulu's Christmas Slay Ride. Our Paradise on a Budget host is a member of the choir and invites us to attend. We decide to make a day of it and jump China Walls in between our morning surf and the evening Christmas concert.

With that settled, and my inbox still full of chatter from hopeful matches, it's Mr. Moped who's call I end up taking on Saturday afternoon. This is the second encounter I describe earlier when I first introduce Mr. Moped. While I wait for him to come over, I spend a few minutes cleaning up my room and repacking my belongings since I won't have much time on Sunday, and I'll be working most of the day Monday before my final sunset dinner on the island with Mr. Erickson. Even though this encounter with Mr. Moped is sexy and judgement-free, I am left unfulfilled, again, with nothing but cum on my face. It's a reminder that I can and should hold out for so much more from my matches.

Despite feeling insatiable, as if there isn't sufficient attention or sex or pleasure or love in the world to meet my needs, I chase matches and links all across the country, unchained and off the rails for the better part of the past year. It is all of a sudden clear to me that this may be a complex form of self-harm. A constantly spinning, partially loaded chamber with the barrel pressed to my temple–each STI test an empty round of negative results, each random hotel or house a close call with an episode of Forensic Files, and it's almost as if I won't be happy until I'm damaged or dead. Exactly what my ex-husband always wanted.

It's like a bolt of introspection when I realize that he still manipulates and controls me through a decade of conditioning where I learn to hate myself as much as he hates me. His iron grip isn't broken even when it's severed. There is more healing that needs to happen before I can truly consider an actual relationship with another man. Perhaps all these mismatched connections are just symptoms of the trauma of my marriage and divorce.

CHAPTER 20

A LEAP INTO THE FUTURE

J ust like most other Sundays since we first met, Kyle and I meet up early at Moku Surf Shop in Waikiki. It's 7 am when we rent boards and walk across Kalakaua Avenue to Waikiki beach to catch waves. It is December 4–just two days before I leave for the mainland so I can be there for my son's birthday, as promised, and for Christmas in Florida with my mom. There is virtually no surf. We hang out in the ocean as the sun climbs into the early morning sky and decide we'll bail early.

We catch the bus to the east side with enough time to grab an açaí bowl from his favorite spot, Café Manoa before we head out to China Walls. After we eat, we walk the mile down to the vacant cul de sac and follow the trail down to the cliffs. Despite his relatively close proximity–the property where Kyle rents his room is just up the road–he hasn't heard of this place. It's not vacant today but there are surprisingly few people there given the nearly flat ocean and perfect jumping conditions. We scope out the ocean for a few minutes and watch the smattering of visitors navigating the cliffs, some of them clearly fresh from their own jumps into the ocean.

Kyle is a lot like my dad. He never met a stranger. Everyone is just a friend he hasn't met yet, so he starts up a conversation with other jumpers to ask about the conditions. They are just as perfect as they look. Before we jump, we agree to take video of each other making the jump. He goes first.

When it's my turn, I spend just a minute grounding myself, feeling the earth beneath my feet, reflecting deeply on my current station in life, the circumstances that brought me here, and with more fear than usual, masked with jokes and a smile, I leave it all behind and leap –

EPILOGUE

It's up to you to decide what parts of this are art and which parts are fiction.

ACKNOWLEDGEMENTS

Thank you to my beta readers–dear friends and relatives–for candid feedback, to Mr. Oxford Comma, for contributions to the grammar and punctuation across the content, and to Sir V, for always keeping it real with me. And gratitude to my mother for telling her own stories, even when she probably wishes she kept those to herself.

ABOUT THE AUTHOR

Hannah Evanstead is the pseudonym of an IT consultant who lives in Honolulu, Hawaii. They are a FaceTime parent to two school-age children who live with their dad in the Midwest state where she originated. In the end, she turned out to be the better of two children from rural, small-town America.

A lover of the performing arts, and especially live music, she's follower of the Grateful Dead, Dead & Co., and Phish. She's a certifiable Phish Chick, the Co-Orgy-Nizer of DickSwap2.0, and an avid disc golfer. She recently added cliff jumping, surfing, and scuba diving to her list of hobbies. Her dating profile can be found on Facebook, Facebook Dating, Hinge, and BLK, but not Tinder, because she is banned.

Made in the USA
Monee, IL
14 July 2023

39258849R00154